# SUTTON'S SCOUNDREL

## THE SINFUL SUTTONS BOOK FIVE

SCARLETT SCOTT

**Sutton's Scoundrel**

The Sinful Suttons Book 5

All rights reserved.

Copyright © 2022 by Scarlett Scott

Published by Happily Ever After Books, LLC

Edited by Grace Bradley

Cover Design by Wicked Smart Designs

This book or any portion thereof may not be reproduced or used in any manner whatsoever without the express written permission of the publisher except for the use of brief quotations in a book review.

The unauthorized reproduction or distribution of this copyrighted work is illegal. No part of this book may be scanned, uploaded, or distributed via the Internet or any other means, electronic or print, without the publisher's permission. Criminal copyright infringement, including infringement without monetary gain, is punishable by law.

This book is a work of fiction and any resemblance to persons, living or dead, or places, events, or locales, is purely coincidental. The characters are productions of the author's imagination and used fictitiously.

For more information, contact author Scarlett Scott.

https://scarlettscottauthor.com

*For my first grade teacher, who first encouraged my love of writing. And for all teachers who find that spark in their students and nurture it.*

# CHAPTER 1

LONDON, 1816

*The* lady was trouble.

Wolf Sutton knew it the moment she crossed the threshold of the office he and his brothers kept at The Sinner's Palace.

For one thing, she was bloody well wearing *white* kid slippers and matching pure-as-snow gloves in the East End. A cove just had to take one glance at her to know she was expensive. She looked as if she were dressed for a ball, in a creamy, gauze gown with a blush-pink layer beneath, the entire affair adorned by satin flowers. An embroidered shawl was wrapped tightly around her shoulders as if it were armor, and she had pearls at her ears and throat. Her brown hair was swept away from her heart-shaped face, with perfect curls framing her loveliness beneath the brim of a bonnet.

For another thing, and her impractical togs aside, she was damned beautiful.

Beautiful morts were *always* trouble. Which was why Wolf stayed far, far away from them. Unfortunately, he could not stay far away from this one. She had invaded his territory. And for a reason, he reckoned.

Best to figure out what it was so he could send her on her merry way. It was not every day that a lone woman who wasn't a Drury Lane vestal cozened her way into The Sinner's Palace's inner sanctum. Ladies of easy virtue were to be had aplenty when there was the chance of attracting a cull with a fat purse. But the woman before him, boldly facing him after having demanded an audience—much to the dismay of one of his best guards—was no harlot. He'd wager the last farthing to his name on that.

"Are you lost, my lady?" he guessed, sweeping an appreciative gaze over her, yet remaining where he was, standing behind his brother's desk, hands clasped at his back.

How the devil had her slippers remained so pure after traversing the rotten streets outside? And what manner of lady would dare to infiltrate a well-known gaming hell? *Alone?*

"This is The Sinner's Palace, is it not?" she returned.

Her voice was serene and yet bore a hint of husky depth that had as unwanted an effect on him as her appearance did. Her aristocratic accent was crisp and educated in a way his own could never hope to be, regardless of the effort at hiring tutors their elder brother had gone to for Wolf and his siblings. The tarnish of the East End would forever mar him—it would mar them all. Strange he had never given a scrope about that until this moment.

Until *her.*

And that didn't sit well in Wolf Sutton's soul. No, indeed.

Nettled, he pinned her with a glare. "Don't know. You tell me where you think you are, madam."

Her eyes narrowed. Not much. Just a hint.

He'd irritated her.

*Bleeding excellent. Because she has more than irritated me.*

"I *know* I am at The Sinner's Palace, sir," she said coolly. "I gave my coachman the direction myself. Shockingly enough, I am capable of simple geography."

Her tone had turned tart, bearing a tone of governess-like admonishment.

It was not meant to have the effect it had on him, he was sure, and he was also damned glad for the barrier of the desk keeping her from seeing what her prim chastisement was doing to his wayward prick. Clearly, the time had come to put an end to living the life of a monk. Just not with the tempting beauty before him. She needed to be dispensed with swiftly and efficiently.

Aye, she needed to go the bloody hell back to the ballrooms and drawing rooms where she so obviously belonged.

"If you know where you've landed, then allow me to guess the reason for your call," he said. "You've come in search of your husband."

And what a pity that was. He knew a hint of envy for the nameless, faceless nob, to have such a lovely woman in his bed.

An elegant brow arched. "I am a widow, sir."

It was wrong, the instant balm of relief he knew at her correction. The lady's husband was gone to Rothisbones, after all. But not even Wolf's conscience could seem to banish the unworthy feeling.

"A lover, then."

"No."

She had neither husband nor lover. The discovery should not please him nearly as much as it did.

He glowered at her, resenting the intrusion on both his solitude and his thoughts. "Forgive me, but you don't look the sort to come looking to ply her wares."

This time, both her eyebrows rose. "Ply her wares? Pray tell me you are not suggesting what I fear you are, sir."

"That you're a public ledger?" he asked, being as crude as possible just because he could not resist the urge to unsettle her as she had done to him. "Don't know. Are you?"

He cocked his head, perusing her with a long, thorough leer. She was bleeding beautiful, this woman.

"A public ledger?" she repeated, her countenance haughty. "I am afraid I do not understand."

She had the airs of a duchess. The urge to further vex her was strong. He had the most ridiculous thought of what it would be like to peel her free of the layers of respectability. He would begin with that shawl. Work his way to the tapes on her gown...

*Stop this madness, you blockhead.*

"A lady of easy virtue," he elaborated. "There are certain sorts of molls who venture through these doors, that being the most common."

Color rose to her high cheekbones and her nostrils flared. "Do you make a habit of insulting your patrons?"

He grinned, enjoying himself. "You ain't a patron."

There was something about his unexpected guest that was compelling. It was not merely her beauty that drew Wolf, though that was plain enough. There was a lively intelligence sparkling in her emerald eyes, an undeniable bravado in her proud bearing that he couldn't help but to admire.

"I could be," she countered.

"We don't allow morts at the tables, no matter how pretty they are. There's a gaming establishment for ladies not far, the Lady Fortune. Seeing as how you're capable of simple geography, you ought to be able to give the directions to your coachman." Wolf could not deny himself the pleasure of throwing some of her lofty words back at her.

"A clever fellow, are you not?" Her tone was dry as she pinned him with a discerning stare that only served to make him harder.

*Damn*, but her ice set him ablaze. He had never, in all his days, experienced anything like it.

"If I were truly clever, I'd throw you over my shoulder and carry you out of here so I can continue with my day," he said coolly, attempting to suppress his reaction.

But it would not abate. And neither would the brazen widow who had infiltrated his office retreat as she ought.

Her expression turned pugnacious. "I dare you to try it, sir."

Well, bleeding hell.

She had challenged him, and now he would have to show her that Wolf Sutton was a man of action. He had never carted a noblewoman out of The Sinner's Palace whilst sporting a cockstand before, but there was a first for every occasion.

∼

DEAR HEAVENS, he was moving toward her. The broad-shouldered, long-legged, hulking wall of man who had stolen her breath when she had first spied him was stalking in Portia's direction, intent clear in every line of his well-muscled form. What was he going to do if he caught her?

And why did the notion of his hands on her send a distressing bolt of heat straight to her core?

"You dare me, do you?" His voice was a low growl that made her belly tighten as if it were a knot being drawn.

Yes, she had, had she not? Because she was a Bedlamite. Only someone in complete dearth of all her logic and sense would have traveled to the East End, brazened her way inside a gaming hell, and then taunted a brawny beast of a man to throw her over his shoulder.

But no hope for it now. She had done all those things. And she had come here for a reason.

Portia defied the instinct that told her to turn and flee while she could, remaining where she was as the man reached her. "Yes. I dare you, sirrah."

He was a tall man, which was refreshing and, she could not deny, appealing. She was accustomed to towering over most of the men in her acquaintance. But this man, this East End rogue with wavy, dark hair and a proud chin and strong jaw and hazel eyes that had swept over her body like a caress, he was only a scant inch taller than she. Their gazes connected as he stood before her, bold and—she loathed to admit—distressingly handsome in a rugged, unpolished way. In a way that made her heart leap in her breast.

"If milady insists."

There was that voice again, deep and pleasant. It was a voice she imagined would be well-suited to telling a lady wicked things. His baritone twined around her, laden with the promise of untold sins.

Oh, she was being fanciful now.

Big hands grasped her waist, seizing her in a grip that was surprisingly gentle for his brutish size and apparent strength. No man had ever touched her there, holding her thus, and that this stranger should be the first—and worse, that she *liked* it—ought to be cause for alarm.

His nearness was intoxicating.

She licked lips that had gone dry. "I did not give you leave to be so familiar with my person."

A slow grin hitched up the corner of his lips, causing her to note how very finely formed they were. "'Course you did, madam. You dared me to throw you over my shoulder. I'm a busy man with much to do this evening. Trifling with petticoats ain't one of them. Seems the most efficient action is to accept your offer."

The way he said *offer* filled her with fire. A longing she

had not experienced in years blossomed. All the yearning she had so ruthlessly suppressed chose that moment to return.

For this man.

This dangerous stranger.

She did not even know his name.

It did not matter. Portia placed her gloved hands atop his, thinking to remove his touch. But the heat of him seared her through the barrier of soft kid. And the scent of him, musk and citrus, so sensual and unexpectedly alluring, hit her. He was raw power, harsh, masculine beauty, and she had never, not since her days as a reckless debutante who believed the world rested in the palm of her hand, wanted to kiss a man more than she wanted to kiss him. The realization stunned her.

Robbed the breath from her lungs for the second time. Stole her ability to speak. Banished her determination.

*I must remember why I am here*, she urged herself sternly. *I must think of Avery.*

Yes, Avery was the reason she had come. The unexpected call from Mrs. Courteney had led her here to The Sinner's Palace in the hope that she would find some answers, or at least a whisper of a hint of something, *anything* about where he may be.

But then, the man's head dipped, his delicious mouth hovering just over hers, and she forgot about her reason for venturing to The Sinner's Palace in furtive fashion just before the ball Granville had insisted she attend. Forgot about everything but the maddening stranger and the desire suddenly coursing through her traitorous body.

"Are you going to do it?" she asked, her voice huskier than she would have preferred, marked with hunger.

Because all she was truly thinking about was him kissing her. His lips on hers.

And then, somehow, her fanciful imaginings became reality. His mouth joined with hers, hot and surprisingly soft. The jolt of awareness that surged through her was unprecedented. She had not felt so much from a simple kiss in…

*Ever.*

She had never felt so wild, so alive, so desperately seeking and needing.

Not even the kisses that had enticed her to ruin years ago had possessed such an effect upon her. Suddenly, she was ravenous for more. Her hands fled his, no longer protesting his grasp on her waist but twining around his neck instead. One swift step forward, and her body molded to his sturdy frame, her breasts crushed to his wide chest. His heat and strength enveloped her as he wrapped her in an embrace that was at once protective and possessive.

*This is where I belong.*

The giddy realization was utter foolishness. Likely borne from the lonely, proper widow's life she had been living. To say nothing of the cold marriage she had endured as penance for her youthful follies.

Thoughts of Blakewell inevitably subdued some of her ardor, chasing her enjoyment of the moment. The stranger kissing her must have taken note of the tensing of her body, for he abruptly pulled his lips from hers. Her mouth instantly mourned the loss of the fiery connection, the fierce pressure of his lips molding over hers.

To her relief, he did not withdraw entirely. Instead, he remained as he was, holding her tightly and yet not too tightly, near enough that his breath—gratifyingly ragged—passed hotly over her mouth.

"Forgive me," he said. "It was not my intention to kiss you."

How could he know the withering of her passion had not been caused by him, but rather by the insidious ghosts of her past, never far from her heels? He could not.

Somehow Portia knew, to her very marrow, that if she allowed her beautiful stranger to retreat, she would never again know his kiss. And for reasons she did not dare examine, she could not bear for that to happen.

The old Portia returned.

The wicked wanton.

The one who had allowed her passions to rule her.

The girl she had thought long buried.

*Lady Scandal.*

Because instead of disengaging and accepting his apology, instead of allowing him to accept all the blame for their sudden, fervent kiss, she slipped her gloved fingers into his too-long hair. Grasped a handful and held him there, where she wanted him.

"I believe it was *I* who kissed *you*, sir," she said, denying him the right to claim the passion that had sparked to life, refusing to allow him to so summarily dismiss it.

Because she wanted—*craved*—more.

"Wolf," he growled.

For a moment, she feared she had mistaken him. She blinked, dazed by a powerful combination of desire and shock at her own wayward actions, her response. "Wolf?"

"My name." A smile curved his lips, revealing a straight line of teeth, a slight, charming gap between the front two. "It's Wolf. Not *sirrah*. Not *sir*. Wolf."

*Good heavens*, he had the name of a beast.

She ought to be appalled. It was a ridiculous name. A name no gentleman in her circles would proudly call his own. And yet, it suited him.

"Wolf," she repeated, trying it on her tongue. He was a stranger no more, then. For he had a name.

"Aye." The grin widened, his hazel eyes—gray and green with flecks of copper and gold—searing into her. "Better. If you kiss me, you ought to at least know that, just as I should know yours, milady."

She should tell him a different name. Fears of Granville and what he would do should he discover she had come to a gaming hell alone and kissed a baseborn man she had not even been introduced to, cautioned her not to tell this man —*Wolf*—her true name.

And yet, it seemed a sin to besmirch the undeniable attraction burning between them with a lie.

"Portia," she said.

And what was the harm? London was likely teeming with at least a dozen Portias, if not more. She had not told him she was the widowed Countess of Blakewell. He knew nothing of her, aside from her given name and her face. And where were their paths ever likely to cross, apart from her lone excursion to this gaming hell?

*Nowhere.*

"Portia." One of his hands moved from her waist, sliding to her lower back, anchoring her to him. "Fitting name."

Did he mean it as an insult or as praise? She could not tell. It hardly signified.

Because in the next moment, he added, "My turn, then."

And his lips were on hers. Fiery and demanding, working over hers as if he sought not just to pleasure her, but to consume her. Ravishing kisses. That was what they were. And he had yet to use his—

*Oh.*

There it was, his tongue, parting her lips for his advance. Portia's fingers tightened in his hair as she opened for him, returning his kiss with all the fervor roiling through her. A small cry emerged from her, a needy whimper. Her nipples were hard and aching, and between her legs, she was throbbing with desire that had been suppressed for far too long.

Or mayhap that wasn't the reason for her fierce reaction. Mayhap it was just *him*.

The hand that had lingered at her waist slid to her hip, cupping her there, drawing her more firmly against his body as he plundered her mouth. And she found herself hooking her leg around his, wishing the cumbersome barrier of her gown did not exist. Her tongue mated with his. It was the most feral, hedonistic, raw kiss she had ever shared with another.

It was the prelude to his cock deep inside her.

Portia had lost her innocence long ago, and to a man who had not deserved the love she had given him. But experience meant she knew what she wanted, what she needed. She wanted Wolf, surname unknown. Wanted his body on hers, inside her. Wanted him to take her to the massive carved desk he had been standing behind at her earlier entrance. Wanted him to raise her gown and petticoats and chemise, to align his cock to her cunny, and sink deep inside. To take her fast and hard. To make her spend.

It had been so long—far too long—since any man had made her feel so alive.

And although it was wrong, so very wrong, and forbidden and against every vow she had made to herself, she could not deny how badly she wanted this man now. She should put an end to this madness. And she would. But first, just one more kiss.

One more kiss.

And another...

She was lost in him.

# CHAPTER 2

*H*e was lost in her.

Lost in his mystery woman who had intruded upon the calm quiet of his evening with the seductive fury of a mythical Siren. She was calling him to the rocks. Calling him to disaster.

And he did not give a bloody goddamn.

Wolf prided himself on his restraint. He had been tempted many times. He'd been born and raised in the rookeries, and Wolf had been presented with the sordid opportunities which inevitably offered themselves. But nothing about the lady in his arms felt sordid. And not one thing about the sweet, seductive play of her mouth against his was like any kiss that had preceded it.

He had always stopped before temptation led him astray. Because unlike his father, Wolf believed in duty. And his duty was to his family, the Suttons. To his siblings, their collective livelihood, the thriving and ever-growing business empire they had built and grown together. Petticoats were a distraction he did not require and could not afford. He had believed himself in love once, and what a bleeding fool he had been.

The sting and the bitterness of his youthful folly had taught Wolf everything he needed to know.

He had a perfectly able hand, and he employed it regularly, to much satisfaction.

Which was why he *never* did what he was doing now, feeding off a woman's mouth as if his very life depended upon it, his hands roving her body as if she were his to please. He was perfectly content to watch over The Sinner's Palace, tend to his family as they needed, and distract himself with physical exertion that involved neither quim nor faithless hearts.

So why could he not stop? What was it about this lady, whose full name he did not even know, whose business here at The Sinner's Palace remained shadowy and unspoken, this widow with her pristine kid gloves and slippers and her ball gown and jewels, that made him want to take her in his arms and carry her away to his bed? A bed where he had never taken another. What was it about her that made him long to keep her there all night? To eschew every responsibility, all the warning within his very soul for this woman?

*Portia.*

Her name was Portia.

It was lovely and elegant and clearly the name of a lady, just as her dress and manners suggested she was. But despite that and his own determination to avoid all entanglements, Wolf was kissing her. Her breasts were full and lush, crushed into his chest, her hip a decadent curve molded perfectly to his palm. And her response to him.

Lord God, *her response.*

She was kissing him as if she were desperate for him, as if she were starved for the feeling of his lips, as if she were breathing him in and out. Her mouth was hungry and skilled, hot and lush, and the answering lust she inspired in him was not just voracious, but heady. She was making needy little sounds low in her throat. Her fingers clutched at him, her nails biting into his flesh through the layers of civility separating them, tongue mating with his in a furor of longing that threatened to bring him to his knees.

They were moving.

Wolf could not be certain which of them initiated the advance. Perhaps it was mutual. All he did know was that they were traveling over the sumptuous carpets, their lips never parting, their kisses unending. Headed for the desk. Lurching into the damned thing, actually.

In a daze of desire, he realized the pain in his hip was the bite of the massive, carved desk connecting with flesh and bone. Not even the ache was enough to stop him. Whether it was the spur of her eager hands passing over his body, the throaty mewls as they kissed, or the nature of this meeting, her identity cloaked in mystery, he could not say.

But he was beyond the point of stopping himself.

Wolf caught her waist in his hands and lifted her until her rump was on the desk. Without breaking their kiss, he found her gown and petticoats, crumpling fabric in his fists, raising the layers up her calves, past her knees. And there he lingered, for he had forever been helpless to resist the forbidden allure of the sheltered bend behind a lady's knee. He had not often had occasion to caress a woman thus; indeed, only one had preceded her, but paradise awaited.

His fingers dipped into the warmth, and though her silken stockings kept him from the soft flesh he longed for, her moan of need spurred him on. He caressed higher, skimming over her garters, and finally found the glory of her skin. Supple and smooth and curved. Her thighs parted in an invitation he readily accepted, drawn to the blazing heat of her cunny.

Wolf was about to go too far, and he knew it. But her arms wound around his neck, holding him tight to her, and she deepened the kiss, sucking on his tongue. The act, so lewd and hungry, could not help but to make him think of her mouth elsewhere. He groaned and pressed his aching cock against the desk between her legs, seeking relief and finding none. Not even the sharp hardness of the wood could provide sufficient distraction.

All he could think, all he could feel, all he wanted was *her*. More of her.

And the beckoning warmth radiating from her quim.

*Quim.*

He was a scant inch from the heart of her, and the urge to see her was every bit as fierce as the need to touch. He wanted to stroke her silken flesh, to discover how wet she was. To make her writhe and moan with desire. But he also wanted to *look*. To feast his eyes on the sight of her flushed and disheveled on the desk, lips swollen from his kisses, her hems raised, thighs open. If he was going to go this far, he wanted everything, wanted to become drunk on her.

It was reckless and wrong, going against every guiding principle that had led him through his life thus far. He had no notion of why of all the women in London, this one should tempt him beyond control, but she did. Her boldness, her beauty, the rightness of her curves aligned so sweetly to his body—he had no notion. It hardly mattered.

Why had he been waiting?

Who had he been waiting for?

In this moment, it seemed irrevocable that he had been waiting for her, for this mysterious lady who had barged into his world and kissed him first. This gorgeous goddess of a brunette whose height nearly matched his and who kissed with such potent eloquence that he thought he could cheerfully spend the rest of his days doing nothing but worshiping her mouth.

All questions died when his touch slid unerringly higher,

to the apex of her thighs. Taking command of the kiss, he cupped her mound, a surge of possession unlike any he had ever known colliding with the desire. She might as well have been fashioned of flame, for her heat seared him, and the dew seeping from her bathed his fingertips.

Wolf could not resist.

His middle finger stroked up and down her seam, dipping between her plump folds where she was even slicker and hotter. His seeking digit found her entrance. She moaned into his mouth and her hips jerked as he lightly circled her there, taunting them both with light pressure, nothing more than his fingertip driving against her in a slow, shallow thrust.

*More.*

It was a litany in his mind. A pounding in his heart. His entire chest was seized in the grip of something indefinably wondrous, as if he were going to fly out of his skin at any moment.

*More, more, more.*

His prick was harder than a marble bust, rising to rude prominence against the desk, and it felt so bloody good—everything felt so damned good—that he rocked against the piece of furniture, as if he were fucking her instead of a lifeless hunk of carved wood. Like a simple-minded beast, he pressed nearer. He followed her slit as he finally tore his lips from hers, burying his face in her throat, where she was soft and floral scented and her pulse beat a frantic rhythm against his questing mouth. He opened, tasting her sweetness on his tongue, sucking her creamy skin until she sighed.

Wolf told himself he was not going to tup her. He was not going to drop the fall of his trousers and align his aching cock to her dripping cunny. Was not going to push inside her. Was not going to smash his every good intention to disastrous bits by joining his body with hers.

He had waited this long to bed a woman.

He would not have his first experience here, on the desk he shared with his brothers at the family gaming hell, with a woman whose surname he did not know. With a lady. A woman who was clearly his better. A woman who could have been anyone.

Not just anyone, he acknowledged then as his finger found the swollen bud he sought. *Portia.* Her name was Portia, and her hips danced on the desk when he played with her pearl and a seductive gasp tore from her as he applied a bit more pressure, working her back and forth. She came with another cry, riding his fingers as he continued to tease her.

*More. Give me more.*

Her name was Portia, and he was going to sink his cock deep inside her drenched cunny and fuck her until he forgot about everything but—

The sound of the door opening cut through the haze of desire threatening to drown him.

His reaction was swift. He removed his hand and flipped down her skirts, spinning around, careful to place himself between Portia and whomever had dared to intrude. His brother Hart, as it happened.

Hart's brows rose. "I didn't expect you to be…within."

Wolf's ears went hot at the implication. Had his brother been making a bloody terrible joke? It hardly mattered.

He struggled to control himself, to regain composure and catch his breath.

"What are you doing here?" he demanded, when at last he found his voice. "Thought you were courting."

Hart was the last of Wolf's brothers to marry—aside from Loge. Supposing Loge was unwed. No one knew the answer to that question, and Logan wasn't speaking to any of them.

And Hart was in the process of wooing Lady Emma Morgan, his betrothed.

Hart eyed him with a barely contained smirk. "I've an hour before the appointed time to pay a call. Em's Aunt Rosamund is bleeding particular about these matters. Care to introduce me to your *friend*?"

Portia grabbed a fistful of Wolf's coat at the small of his back, the desperate warning clear. The lady wished to remain anonymous. And Wolf could scarcely blame her.

He crossed his arms over his chest, willing his heart to cease galloping and the lust to die a hasty death. "No."

His brother, however, being the arsehole he was, was rather reminiscent of a dog with a bone. Perhaps repayment for the taunts Wolf had admittedly issued to Hart concerning ladies, the parson's mousetrap, and falling in love.

Because Hart lingered instead of departing, grinning. "Hugh didn't tell me you had petticoats in here or I'd have waited. It ain't like you."

His brother was right, and he hated it. Having a wench here at The Sinner's Palace wasn't like him at all. Indeed, aside from Lydia, he had never willingly brought another woman beneath this roof. Had never bedded a woman, either. Not that he had not been tempted before. He had. But his convictions had always been far stronger than the need to lose himself in a woman's body.

*This one ain't like the rest.*

He cleared his throat, tamping down the voice within, the acknowledgment that there was something about Portia which made her stand apart from every woman he had known. "Sometimes we all do things that ain't like us. Courting, for instance."

Hart's eyes narrowed, the only sign Wolf's barb had found its mark. "Aye, brother. I will leave you to conduct your business then."

With a curt nod, Hart stepped out of the office, closing the door behind him and leaving Wolf and Portia once more alone. The interruption had been enough to quash his raging lust and to invite a return to reason. Wolf faced the woman who had so unexpectedly turned his evening asunder.

Her cheeks were flushed, and her bonnet was askew, tendrils of dark hair having come free of her coiffure to curl around her cheeks. Her emerald-green eyes were luminous as she avoided his gaze, her gloved hands rearranging the fall of her skirts, not without a telling tremble. Her mouth was kiss-bruised and the sweet shade of crushed summer berries, and the urge to put his lips on hers once more took him by surprise with its sudden ferocity.

She slid from the desk, her slipper-shod feet landing with a demure thud. "I must apologize."

The cool elegance had returned to her voice, her bearing. It was as if the conflagration between them had never burned. As if she had not sealed her mouth with his and sucked his tongue, as if his fingers were not still wet with the evidence of her desire.

Delicious evidence.

His thumb, forefinger, and middle finger rubbed together, slick from her dew, and despite his deeply held notion of honor and his vow to himself that he would never allow a woman to lead him astray again, he burned with the need to touch her once more. Longed to guide her back to the desk, to kiss her, raise her hems, and slide his hand between her thighs to reassure himself the decadent silk of her cunny and the throbbing bud of her pearl had been real.

"Why apologize?" he asked her, although he knew damned well he should not.

Instead, he should allow her to gather her pride and flee. Rest easy in the knowledge that he would never see her again. That this wild and reckless passion had been a passing thrill he would soon forget.

Her gaze flicked to his, and he felt it as if it were a caress. "It was not my intention to behave with such a shocking absence of morals. I can assure you that I do not... I have not acted so injudiciously in years."

He was not sure if he should be pleased or disappointed by this news.

Wolf remained still, refusing to retreat but instead remaining near, lingering in the spell that her luscious, floral scent had cast upon him. "You have before, then?"

She blinked. "I have what?"

"Acted injudiciously." And she had done so with another. Years ago, apparently. That part rather stung, and he could not say why. The notion that someone else, some faceless, nameless nob, had been the recipient of her potent kisses and sensual allure nettled him.

For the brief span of time he had held her in his arms, how easy it had been to pretend she was his.

Her tongue slid over her lips, the jerky inhalation of her breath drawing his attention to her throat where he had inadvertently left his mark on her in his reckless enthusiasm. And damn, but the sight of her skin reddened from his mouth and the scrape of his whiskers abrading the sensitive flesh was enough to make his cock begin to harden again.

"I have made many mistakes in my life, Mr...."

"Just Wolf," he supplied, the ice in her voice enough to kill his rising ardor. Wolf took a step back and offered her a mocking bow. "I trust your presence 'ere is an aberration. Whatever the reason you mistakenly gave your coachman this direction, you've realized you don't belong, and you'll not be returning."

His voice was harsher than he had intended. The color fled her cheeks and her chin went up, her lush mouth tightening, making him regret the lash of his response. But bleeding hell, he would not be any woman's mistake.

Never again.

Without awaiting Portia's response, he turned his back on her and stalked from the room. One of the guards, Hugh, was lurking in the hall, and Wolf asked him to see the unexpected guest to her coachman unscathed. It was the best he could do. All the time he was willing to waste on any woman. He had already come perilously close to forgetting the vow he'd made to himself long ago when Lydia had given his heart such a drubbing, she'd left it nothing more than ash.

He didn't need any woman causing trouble or bringing him temptation. Especially not one who was a lady and regretted lowering herself by welcoming his touch and kiss.

As he strode to the gaming rooms to check the floor, Wolf told himself he had done the right thing. He'd never know the reason why she had come to The Sinner's Palace or what she had been seeking, but it hardly mattered. What *did* matter was that he would never see her again.

# CHAPTER 3

"His lordship, the Marquess of Granville, is calling, my lady."

Portia bit her inner lip to keep from wincing in dread at the butler's announcement that her odious brother had chosen to pay a call. She had known Granville would. Indeed, she had spent much of the night before sick with dread after she had been too flustered from her visit to The Sinner's Palace to attend the ball as he had expected of her.

However, she had not supposed he would arrive at this early hour, and the very next day, instead of merely sending a strongly worded missive expressing his displeasure. Apparently, her lack of obedience had heralded the need for a vicious upbraiding face-to-face. Her hands trembled as she pulled the needle through her embroidery and set it aside in a basket.

She pinned what she hoped was a serene smile to her face as she rose to her feet. "Please see his lordship in, Riggs."

With a bow, the butler took his leave, allowing Portia a few frantic moments to prepare herself for the distasteful interview which was bound to follow. The cheerful sun slanting through the windows of the sitting room where she preferred to spend her mornings provided no comfort. The care she had taken in decorating the chamber was lost on her now.

After Blakewell's death, she had, for the first time, begun to make her mark upon the town house. She had spent her marriage being made to feel a guest, forever reminded of the good fortune which had fallen into her lap, saving her from ruin. Her life in exchange for her son's. Despite the cold, unhappy marriage she had shared with Blakewell, Portia did not regret her decision. Given the chance, she would do the same, if it meant giving Edwin the life he deserved.

And now, here was her turn, with her period of mourning at an end, to live a bit of the life she deserved. At least, as much as the rigid strictures placed on her would allow. She had chosen to express herself in the decoration of her home. Elegant paper-hangings, pictures painted by artists of her choice rather than the staid representations of generations of earls and countesses long gone. A writing desk situated by the window, where she happily conducted her correspondence in the glow of the natural light. Books on a small shelf that were of interest to her alone...

"Sister."

Granville's presence at the threshold, coupled with the frigid disapproval in his voice, was enough to chase her from her brief, fanciful enjoyment of her surroundings.

She dipped into a curtsy. "Lord Granville."

Formality was of the utmost import to her brother, and since he was the guardian Blakewell had appointed for her son, Portia had no choice other than to live her life according to Granville's expectations.

"I understand you were ill yesterday evening," he said, venturing into the room just near enough that he would not be forced to conduct their conversation with the chance of servants overhearing.

A sliver of relief slid through her. If he was not close, and if the door to the sitting room remained open, then perhaps she would be spared the punishment he often chose to inflict in his moments of rage.

"Yes," she said calmly, agreeing with the lie she had sent as her excuse, hoping he did not hear the tremor in her voice.

Prevarication was a sin Granville did not tolerate. Along with fornication without the bonds of marriage. And ruining herself by allowing a lord to steal her virtue. Naturally, Landringham, as Granville's friend, had never been made to suffer for his sins as Portia had. The woman always bore the burden in such matters, as Mother had fretfully explained when she had discovered Portia's courses had failed to arrive.

Clasping his hands behind his back, her brother stalked deeper into the room, though not before discreetly toeing the door closed. "What manner of illness?"

Her hope that this interview would proceed in a civilized fashion vanished.

She swallowed, trying not to think about the unexpectedly heated, entirely forbidden moments she had shared the evening before with the man she knew only as Wolf. "I was feverish."

That much was true, but not because of any sickness.

Rather, she had been brought to life for the first time in years.

All because of an East End rogue with a tinge of the rookeries in his speech and callused hands that had felt far too good on her bare skin. As if they belonged there.

"Feverish," Granville repeated coldly, his countenance implacable.

It was impossible to determine whether or not he was disappointed or furious with her. Neither boded well.

"Yes." She held her brother's gaze, unflinching, hoping he would not read the lie in her eyes or the guilty warmth she could not help but to feel creeping into her cheeks.

Her mind was filled with sinful remembrances. Wolf's mouth on hers, his tongue sweeping past her lips, his hand, sliding unerringly between her legs. *Dear heavens*, if Granville knew she had been playing the wanton at an East End gaming hell, he would take Edwin from her forever. And that, she could not bear. That, she could not allow.

"Why was I not informed that you were ill until the last possible moment?" His eyes narrowed, suspicion creeping into the harshness of his voice.

*Because I was not ill at all. Indeed, to the contrary, I have never felt better than I did yesterday evening.*

She could not say that. Telling the truth was dangerous. And reckless. As reckless as she had been, years ago. And then again last night.

Portia swallowed. "I did not wish to burden you or Lady Granville."

Her brother's lip curled. "You are dissembling."

Icy tendrils of fear crept into her heart. There was no way he could know she was not telling him the truth. No means by which he could be certain she was being deceptive.

Her chin went up, and it required all the calm she possessed to maintain a placid countenance. "Why should I lie to you, brother? You must forgive me, I pray. I had every intention of attending your ball as you had requested. However, I became so ill that I was concerned I would bring shame upon you. I had no wish to swoon or otherwise act in an untoward manner."

Granville stalked nearer, stopping at her writing desk, trailing an idle finger over the polished surface. "Shame such as that which you brought upon our family when you chose to lie with Landringham outside the bonds of marriage?"

Her jaw clenched, for she hated the old wounds, so easily torn open even after so much time had passed. "Hardly that manner of shame, my lord."

"You went to a den of thieves and whores last night."

His voice was soft. Deceptively so.

The accusation hung in the air.

Everything inside her froze. "No."

She did not know why she denied her presence at The Sinner's Palace. She had taken an unmarked carriage and proceeded with the greatest of care, terror that her brother would discover where she had gone and what she had done leaving her on edge for the entirety of the trip. And she had been certain, so certain, that no one save her coachman and groom had known where she had been. But if Granville suspected she was being dishonest, then he had discovered where she had truly gone.

The reason for his early, unannounced call made itself brutally apparent to her in the same moment that her brother picked up her inkwell and hurled it against the wall. It shattered against the paper-hangings she had chosen, creating a terrible splatter, marring the flocked pattern forever.

"Do not deceive me, Portia," Granville warned.

How did he know? Who had told him? She did not believe it of her coachman or her groom; if she had not trusted them implicitly, she never would have ventured to the East End in search of Avery.

"Those paper-hangings were dear," she said instead of giving her brother the answers he wanted. Where her daring emerged from, she could not say. Portia knew from experience that goading her brother was never wise. And yet, she could not seem to help herself. "I paid for them with my widow's portion."

And a pittance it was, her widow's portion. Granville had

persuaded Blakewell to leave the bulk of his considerable fortune in the hands of her son's guardian, who had also been appointed trustee. Yes, her brother had been sure to yoke her to him, to assert his power over her, for as long as possible. She could only pray that when Edwin reached fourteen, they could bring the matter to the Chancery and her son could request Portia be named as guardian in her brother's stead. However, that was seven long and painful years away, and there was no guarantee such an appeal would succeed.

"The paper hangings are hideous," Granville spat. "But let the mark upon them be a reminder to you of the stain upon your character for the sins you have committed. Sins which, it is apparent, you would revisit."

He was speaking of the past. But he could not have any notion of what she had done in the gaming hell's private office with Wolf. She did not believe he had spies within The Sinner's Palace. No one there had even been told her name. He was making an assumption based upon her presence there. And the spy had to be someone within her household.

She ought to have guessed that her brother would have someone below stairs who would report back to him since Blakewell's death. A year had passed, and she had never given him cause for concern. But the first time she had ventured to the East End, and he *knew*.

"I have done nothing wrong," she denied again, a last attempt.

But there was no hope for it. If she were to reveal what she had done, what she had allowed—nay, what she had craved—Granville would not hesitate to keep her from her son. She would be powerless to fight him. And she could not bear to lose Edwin. Her sweet lad was her very heart.

"Can you truly say you believe it appropriate for a lady to visit a gaming hell in the rookeries?" he snapped.

"I went there looking for Avery," she confessed on a rush, for it was true.

Their half brother was the reason she had gone to The Sinner's Palace. However, she had not found him within. And Avery had not been the reason she had remained for far too long, lingering in sinful temptations.

Granville flinched as if she had struck him. "Avery."

"Our brother," she reminded him quietly.

"He is no brother of mine."

Avery had been more of a brother to her than Granville had ever been. Although his mother had been their father's mistress and he had been born on the wrong side of the blanket, for a charmed few years when Portia had been a girl, she had grown to know and love the brother far closer in age to her. Until he had been torn away from the bosom of their family.

But Portia had not forgotten him. Nor had she ceased searching for him.

"You can deny him all you like Granville, but it will not change the past," she said, trying and failing to conquer her own rising frustration.

Raising her voice to her brother had never ended particularly well for Portia. It led to consequences far worse than an inkwell being hurled at her paper-hangings.

He stalked toward her, closing the distance, looming over her own not-inconsiderable height, his fists clenched at his sides. "You dare to speak to me with such impudence? You, who nearly ruined our family? You, who has the morals of a Seven Dials doxy? You may wear the airs of a proper widowed countess, but make no mistake, everyone remembers the shameless manner in which you conducted yourself in your Season."

His insult did not hurt, because she had heard it before. Many times. His hatred for her was apparent; it had been well before she had ruined herself, but Blakewell's death and Granville's resulting supremacy in her life had left him emboldened. He rained insults and threats upon her with increasing frequency, along with violence.

His fury was dangerous. She had to mollify it. She had intended to explain, but speaking of Avery to him had been a mistake. Better than admitting what she had done in that office. But a mistake, nonetheless.

"Forgive me," she said then, trying to calm the rage rising within him. "I should never have been so bold. It was wrong of me."

Apologies.

Her life had been a series of them. Repenting for her sins. Making amends. Marrying a man who would accept her child as his own. Bending to her brother's power and whims. Living a life above reproach. Keeping her reputation spotless. Making certain she was no longer Lady Scandal, as the gossips had once dubbed her.

But Portia was tired of asking forgiveness for old transgressions. For living each moment of the present as if she were still mired in the past. And yet, she had no choice.

She bowed her head in feigned humility.

The action proved a mistake, for instead of placating Granville as it sometimes had during previous interviews, the action appeared to further infuriate him. Her only warning was a low growl of rage. She flinched, trying to escape, but it was too late. His palm connected with her face in such stinging force she bit her cheek, the tang of her own blood filling her mouth. Her eyes instantly welled with burning tears she refused to shed.

"You will not bring more shame upon this family," he said, his voice low and yet carrying the punishing menace of a whip.

When Granville was truly angered, he was quiet. And that was when he was at his most dangerous and destructive.

She closed her eyes, keeping her head bent, gaze trained on the carpets, her cheek aching. "Of course not. I am sorry."

Yet another apology.

The blow would cause a mark she would need to cover, she knew. Portia preferred the clever application of Pear's Almond Bloom to hiding herself in her chamber. By now, she had become adept at blending it into her skin to cover the damage. Besides, Edwin was of an age where he wondered where his mother had gone, and as her son grew older with each passing year, she found herself less inclined to spend time away from him, knowing too soon he would be sent away from her. Granville had already demanded he go to Eton, and as had been the precedent for nearly all her life, Portia would have no choice in the matter.

"Do you think I take joy in being stern with you?" her brother demanded.

*Yes.*

He had been cruel in his youth, and he had grown into a cruel man. But telling him so would only earn her another slap. Perhaps worse.

She swallowed against the pride that told her to maintain her defiance. "Of course not, my lord."

"I must do it, for your own sake and for the sake of your son."

"Yes," she agreed woodenly.

*Numbly.*

It was best to agree with Granville. She should have attended the ball as he had required of her. But she had been too flustered after her encounter that she had unwisely chosen to flee to the haven of her bed chamber.

"Now, tell me why you thought to find Father's bastard at

a gaming hell in the East End," he said, instead of taking his leave as she had hoped he would.

She did not dare tell him the full truth, and neither did she have the courage to lie. If he knew she had gone to The Sinner's Palace yesterday, then he likely also would have known about Mrs. Courteney's call.

"Avery's mother paid me a visit," she said, carefully refraining from mentioning it had been because Portia had been seeking the woman, hoping she would have some information concerning her brother. "She told me that when last she heard from him, he had been working at a gaming hell, or so she believed. I… I went there believing I might find him."

"You went to the rookeries instead of attending my ball."

The threat in her brother's voice was undeniable. It had been a risk, hastening to The Sinner's Palace yesterday. However, she had been willing to take it, if she would be reunited with the only brother she had ever loved. The only brother who had loved her. She had not forgotten the sweet lad who had shown her how to fish and climb trees and throw a punch, the boy who had protected her from Granville's wrath.

Until, one day, he had simply been gone. No explanation. No warning. Simply *gone*.

"I wished to find him with all haste," she admitted softly now.

"Look at me when you are speaking," Granville demanded.

Willing her tears to subside, she did as he asked, lifting her head and her gaze.

Her brother's jaw was clenched, his expression murderous. "You will never again seek out Avery Tierney, do you understand?"

She nodded, but in her heart, she knew it for the lie it was. One of many, just like her apologies.

"I want to hear the words, sister," he ground out.

If she did not comply, he would strike her again, she knew.

"I will never again seek out Avery Tierney," she repeated.

"I shall inform the household that Mrs. Courteney is to be turned away," he added coldly.

"Of course," she agreed, as if it were the most logical assumption and she were in complete accord.

"You will join us for dinner soon," her brother announced coolly. "Lady Granville was most displeased you failed to attend her ball. She will expect an apology."

Yet another.

Her brother's wife was a cold and cunning woman. Portia had often wondered if Granville resorted to violence with her, but such was their relationship that she did not trust to ask for fear she would go to Portia's brother with the query.

"I will be pleased to join you and to offer my apologies to Lady Granville."

"And you will not return to the rookeries," he added.

"No." Her traitorous mind thought again of the diabolically handsome man at The Sinner's Palace, his kisses, his touch. *Wolf.* A feral name, inherently dangerous and yet, he had kissed and caressed her with deliberate tenderness. No man had ever shown her such care.

And then her heart gave a pang as she thought of Avery. Such a terrible risk she had taken, and then she had squandered it with her wanton ways. She was still no closer to finding her lost brother after fleeing from the gaming hell in a rush of thwarted longing and shame. Perhaps Granville was not wrong about her. Certainly, his loathing for her could not be eclipsed by her own self-disgust.

*Oh Avery, what has become of you?*

"If I discover you are lying to me again, I will take the boy from you," Granville threatened coldly. "Do not think I won't, Portia."

It was the very real possibility he would take Edwin from her, deny her the right to see him and love him, far more than the presage of violence that instilled the most fear in her. Portia could not bear to lose her son. Every other pain was bearable save that one.

"I will not make the mistake again," she promised Granville.

"See that you do not." With a quick, civilized bow that made a mockery of the fury he had just unleashed in her happy little sitting room, her brother took his leave.

## CHAPTER 4

Wolf could not seem to wrest his mystery lady from his mind.

*Portia.*

He had lain awake the night before, hand on his hard cock, stroking himself off to the memory of her hot, silken quim.

Clearing his throat, he shifted on the leather squabs of the carriage, attempting to ease his discomfort and his suddenly aching groin. It would not do to sport a cockstand for which there was no cure whilst he waited for his sister Lily to emerge from Bellingham and Co. He did not particularly appreciate being made to play the chaperone this afternoon. Shopping excursions held about as much interest to him as drinking a steaming cup of horse piss, which was to say none at all.

However, Lily had recently managed to find herself in a dangerous scrape, which had led to Wolf and his siblings deciding their youngest sister required accompaniment aside from the guards at the hell. Along with Hart's betrothed, Lady Emma, Lily had nearly been robbed or worse. That had ultimately led to the discovery that the intrepid Lily had been gallivanting all over London, sometimes *alone.*

Today was Wolf's duty. And he would have been grateful for the distraction and the chance to escape the sometimes suffocating walls of The Sinner's Palace, except that watching over Lily meant sitting in this bleeding carriage with nothing better to do than think about the last woman he ought to be thinking of.

A lady he would most certainly never see again.

Which was for the best, because he had matters of far greater import to attend, such as why the devil their brother Logan had disappeared, only to reappear in the East End calling himself *Mr. Martin* and working alongside the devil's own moneylender, Archer Tierney, doing only Christ knew what. The discovery was yet new, and they were each attempting to make sense of the realization in their own way. While Wolf's initial inclination had been to storm Tierney's establishment demanding answers, Jasper, the eldest and leader of the family, had recommended they proceed with caution, getting their answers through more subtle means.

Wolf sighed and shifted again on the seat. His arse was beginning to get sore from all this damned waiting he was doing. *Floating hell,* what was Lily buying inside the massive brick shop all the quality was atwitter over? Every damned scrap of lace and each bloody feather? His dark mood heightening along with his restlessness, Wolf stared out the window, searching for his sister.

And that was when he saw her.

His Siren from the day before.

He would recognize that tall, shapely form in his sleep after he'd had it beneath his eager hands. Her face was visible in profile, the brim of her bonnet once again keeping him from admiring the full glory of her chestnut hair. It was deuced difficult to believe she was here, almost within reach when he had been so certain their paths would never cross again. And she was going into Bellingham and Co. where Lily was.

He watched as Portia was welcomed when she approached the front façade of the shop. But then, she disappeared within.

Wolf was moving before he had even managed to give the matter coherent thought. He sprang out of the carriage, eating up the distance between himself and his mystery woman with long-legged strides. Thankfully, he had dressed the part of a gentleman today. Whilst he would sooner drown himself in the Thames than be trussed up like a dandy, he could, on occasion, dress with care and affect the airs of his betters.

He was welcomed by an obsequious cove inside the door, who was wondering if he would care to investigate the furs and fans Bellingham and Co. had to offer.

Wolf made a swift choice, flashing the man a smooth smile. "I am seeking my wife. I believe she just passed through the door a few moments before. She was wearing a pale-blue gown with matching bonnet."

There was a chance the man before him would know who Portia was, that he would know she was a widow. But Wolf was in the mood to be bold and take a risk.

"I do believe your wife passed into the haberdashery department," the helpful cove said.

Wolf's grin deepened. "Excellent. If you would direct me there, please?"

The man gestured straight ahead. "That department is to be found just through the first partition, sir."

Once more, his legs were moving. Taking him to her. He had the presence of mind to cast his gaze about in search of Lily, but his sister was nowhere to be seen. He had no notion of what he intended to do when he found Portia. All he knew was that she was near. Her presence at the same shop, at the same time, was too fortuitous to be ignored.

Recklessness had never been one of his traits. And yet, here he was, stalking through Bellingham and Co. on Pall Mall, intent upon finding a woman he knew by first name alone. He spied her immediately upon crossing through the partition into the haberdashery department. Lace, silks, and muslin adorned the walls in an impressive array of wares.

But all Wolf saw was her.

From the periphery of her gaze, she must have taken note of his deliberate movement in her direction, for her head turned. Her green eyes went wide, recognition flaring in their lustrous depths, her lush lips parting on the barest hint of sound.

His name, he thought.

She remembered.

Of course she did.

He reached her side and offered as elegant a bow as he could muster, before proffering his arm. "My lady."

She stared at him in astonishment, not accepting his escort. "What are you doing here?"

He shrugged. "Shopping. What are *you* doing here?"

Her brows snapped together. "Have you followed me?"

A suspicious wench, wasn't she? He wondered why she would instantly guess he might have nefarious motives. Was it because he was a rookeries-born commoner, or was it because something else in her life gave her cause to question? Wolf did not like either notion, but he found he would prefer the former to the latter. Fine ladies who looked down their noses at culls of his ilk were no surprise.

"Why would I do that?" he asked mildly, allowing his gaze to rove over her face and drink her in.

She was achingly lovely. Every bit as beautiful as he had recalled, if not more so. Her emerald eyes were bright, more vibrant than the first grass of spring, or so he fancied. Wasn't much grass to be seen in the rookeries.

"I have no notion," she said coolly, alarm creeping into her voice.

He noted tension in the manner in which she carried herself, her shoulders going stiff. "Because I didn't. Believe it or not, I've better ways to occupy my time than following about ladies who appear at my gaming hell and then disappear with equal haste."

Her gaze traveled about frantically. "You should not be here with me in this fashion, sir."

Back to *sir* again, were they? Formality made him itchy, especially after his hand had been up her skirts.

"Am I not allowed to buy gloves and lace as well as the next cove?" he countered, taunting her when he knew it was unwise.

The lady was clearly disturbed that he had approached her in a space where anyone might see. However, his own cursory inspection of the department revealed a handful of shoppers examining the wares, presided over by a trio of shopkeepers who were seeing to their customers' every whim. No one was paying any attention to Wolf and Portia at all.

His gaze jerked back to hers in time to watch her catch her lower lip between her teeth in a worried nibble. The action revealed her vulnerability, and despite his determination to remain impervious to the woman before him, Wolf knew a pang of regret that he was the one to have caused her discomfiture.

"You came here to buy lace?" she asked, uncertainty edging the sweetly melodic tones of her voice.

Aye, he didn't exactly look like the sort of cull who went about buying lace, did he?

But then, he was not the sole gentleman patron within.

Perhaps the others were purchasing trinkets for their mistresses and wives, or acting as reluctant duennas to their female relatives as he had been.

"No," he answered truthfully, without offering his true reason.

He did not owe this woman an explanation for his presence. Indeed, he ought not to even be standing here with her, near enough to touch her. Lily was about somewhere, and his reason for venturing to Pall Mall was his sister, not Portia.

And yet, all he could think of was not his duty, but kissing the woman who had haunted him all night long. He could not do so, not in public. He may have been born in the rookeries, but he had manners. He knew what was expected of a gentleman, damn it.

"Then you *have* followed me." Her voice was low, laden with accusation.

He had not sought her out to argue with her. *Hell*, he did not know precisely why he had sought her out, but the reason no longer seemed to matter as much as his need to get her somewhere more private. Somewhere they would not be attended by so many eyes and ears.

"I see you have found your wife, sir."

Wolf turned to discover the same annoying, sharp-eyed cove who had greeted him at his entrance had followed him into the haberdashery department, apparently hungry to make certain any purchases Wolf made were attested to him.

The man's irritating manner aside, Wolf found himself relieved the fellow had been so determined. "I have indeed," he said, ignoring the glare of warning Portia aimed at him. "Is there, perchance, a private room where we might view the goods of my lady's choosing?"

"Of course, sir," the man said, eager to be of service. "If you will follow me?"

"We would be delighted." He grinned unrepentantly at Portia, who looked as if she would like to sink a blade between his ribs, and caught her hand, placing it firmly in the crook of his elbow.

"Your wife," Portia muttered. "What have you done?"

"Nothing yet," he reassured her mildly.

*But wait until I have you alone, my dear.*

He did not say that, preferring to keep his plans to himself for now. And to think, merely one quarter hour before, he had been grimly seated in a carriage, awaiting Lily's return, plagued by restlessness and the memories of the lady on his arm. How quick was the turn of fortune's most fickle wheel.

The man led them to a small room which had been built into the perimeter of the haberdashery department. Within, there was a looking glass, a table, and accommodating chairs.

"Tell me, if you please, the items I may bring for your inspection," the man said.

"Thank you," Wolf told him. "The finest gloves you have, a pair in every color, if you please, and some of the lace as well."

The man nodded. "Of course."

With a bow, he discreetly took his leave of the room, closing the door at his back.

It had scarcely snapped closed when Portia released her grip on Wolf's arm and whirled on him, eyes flashing with fire. "What are you about, sirrah? You have taken this game too far."

Bringing her to a private alcove was not nearly as far as he wished to take things between them, and he was rather ashamed to make the realization. It went against every tenet, every guiding principle with which he had ruled his life since Lydia.

But never mind that now. He had Portia. Alone. The

blasted fart sniffer aiding them would be at least five minutes before he returned with the gloves and the lace. Wolf would wager his life on it.

"This ain't a game, love," he said, reaching for her, his hands settling on her waist in a way that felt familiar and right.

He was careful to keep his grasp loose enough that she could disengage with ease if she so chose. She was nettled with him, and whether it was because she had not expected to see him at Bellingham and Co., or whether she truly believed he had somehow followed her here, or if his fib about being her husband had managed to send her into high dudgeon, he didn't know. But he would sooner be dead than force his attentions upon a lady when they were unwelcomed.

Judging from their heated exchange before, they were very much the opposite. However, he was proceeding with care because Portia mattered to him. He swallowed a knot of some unfamiliar emotion at the unwanted acknowledgment.

"You are correct that it is not a game," she told him, her hands settling over his.

However, she kept them there, gloves and civility separating them from bare skin and the sensual connection they had shared the day before.

"Tell me your name." The demand fled his lips without thought, half plea.

Until this moment, he had not believed himself desperate to know who she was and how he might find her again. But he understood it now. This madness between them was deep and visceral. It went beyond lust. He was not prepared to examine the unspoken bond more fully, for fear of what he would discover.

"You already have it," she said, her lips, pretty and pink and so bloody inviting, parting.

"Portia," he agreed, his head dipping just so he could be nearer still, so he could inhale her scent, feel the heat of her breath wafting over his lips in the prelude to a kiss. More madness, he knew. He was queer in the attic. "But that ain't enough. I need to know the rest."

Her gaze searched his, a crease of worry forming between her brows. "You cannot."

She was so deliciously tall. God, he loved that about her. He scarcely even had to bend his head, and he could claim her lips with his. And yet, he was hesitant, for he was not certain how he would be received.

"Why?" Instead of kissing her, he satisfied himself with allowing his right hand to roam from her waist until it was splayed on the small of her back, where the natural curve fitted to his touch. It required all the restraint he possessed to keep from hauling her against him, letting her feel the effect she had on him.

His prick was half-hard, and from nothing at all. Nay, not from nothing.

From *her*.

From the sight of her.

The decadent scent.

Her eyes on his, the warmth of her body, burning into his.

"Because I cannot..." she faltered, her tongue emerging to wet her lips, as if she had grown nervous. "What happened between us was wrong. I cannot indulge in such unbecoming, improper, utterly foolish—"

Wolf ended her diatribe with his lips, for there went his restraint and all his good intentions. Hearing her call what had happened between them yesterday *improper* and *foolish* felt wrong to his marrow. Because kissing her, touching her, had been... Words did not exist which could sufficiently describe it.

The hand at her waist and the one at her back worked in

synchronicity to pull her against him. He angled his mouth over hers, his tongue teasing the seam of her lips. She opened on a sound that was part sigh, part moan, and it went straight to his cock. Her tongue moved against his, and she tasted like pure honey, sweet and delicious, and he did not think he could ever get enough.

Not from a hundred kisses.

Nor a thousand.

He groaned, bringing her nearer still. Her arms went around his neck, clinging, her breasts crushing into his chest. What was it about this woman that brought him to his knees? That made him forget every vow he had made to himself, every pain and hurt he had previously endured, that made him ignore each warning clamoring to be heard within him?

He kissed her and kissed her, their breaths becoming one, her sigh of contentment finding a part of his soul he had long believed turned to ash and bringing it back to life. *Bleeding hell*, if he died tomorrow without ever touching another wench, he would die a happy man to know this woman's lips had been beneath his last.

There was no reason for him to feel such a depth of association.

And yet, he did.

His instinct, however, still remained strong. Being raised in the rookeries left a cove with an undeniable reaction to the slightest unexpected sound. He heard the damned shop cull returning. Footsteps, a discreet knock, followed by the scrape of the latch.

With a muttered curse, he withdrew, setting Portia away from him, and spinning on his heel, he clasped his hands behind his back in time for the door to open. The obsequious cove had returned, arms laden with lace and gloves. With the mountain of goods obstructing his view, the poor fellow likely had no idea what he had just intruded upon.

And Wolf was glad for that, even if he mourned the interruption. Already, he missed her in his arms. Missed her mouth on his.

"Your requests, sir," the man said, helpfully depositing his burden upon the table.

"Thank you," Wolf offered, his voice sounding husky and thick with desire even to his own ears. "If we could have a few moments to examine the wares?"

*Alone.*

That last bit was implied. Wolf didn't know if this was the manner in which a gentleman ordinarily conducted himself at Bellingham and Co. Lord knew he was not one to dabble in purchasing trinkets and trivialities for wenches. And Christ knew he was no gentleman. But he wanted Portia alone, no audience. He would do whatever was required to have it.

"Of course, sir." Another bow, and the shop cove disappeared, leaving the fripperies he had procured behind, the door once more discreetly closed.

Wolf turned back to Portia, admiring the flush in her cheeks and the sparkle in her vivid, green eyes. She looked nettled with him and deliciously well-kissed.

"Your behavior is outrageous, sir," she said.

He gestured to the door. "Leave if you like."

She remained where she was. "Why are you here?"

He fought the urge to grin. "To kiss you."

Her color heightened. "Then you followed me, just as I've said."

"Into this establishment? Aye, that much is true. I was waiting in a carriage when I recognized you." He studied her lovely face, knowing he would see it in his sleep tonight.

A regal brow rose, her shoulders stiffening. "You were awaiting someone, then?"

He nodded, pleased in spite of himself that she appeared troubled by the possibility he was dancing attendance on another lady. "My sister."

"You have a sister?"

This time, he did grin. "You find it so difficult to believe? The quality ain't the only ones with siblings, my lady."

Her lush lips parted. "That is not what I meant to suggest."

They were wasting precious time speaking of things that did not interest him nearly as much as learning her full name and where and when he might see her again did.

Wolf moved nearer, drawn to her as he had been from the moment their gazes had connected the day before at The Sinner's Palace. "What *did* you mean to suggest?"

Her gaze dipped to his mouth, and he knew she was thinking of the kisses they had so recently shared, the same as he was. "I suppose that what I meant was I had not thought of you having a family, a sister for whom you wait whilst she completes her shopping."

"You were thinking of me, then." He longed to touch her, but he restrained himself. He had kissed her first and orchestrated their privacy in this antechamber it was true, but he wanted them to be equals. He needed to be certain she desired him every bit as much as he did her.

Her flush heightened. "Yes," she admitted, the lone word the barest whisper of a sound. "I was thinking of you."

He smiled. "How?"

Her eyes widened, and he thought he could stare into the vibrant, emerald depths for an entire day and still find new shimmering hues within them. Gold, cinnamon, streaks of brown, hints of gray. They were not hazel, not like his, but richer, fancier. Just as she was. And fringed with dark, luxurious lashes that seemed to Wolf to be the most extravagant—and beguiling—eyelashes he'd ever beheld on a woman.

"Do you truly wish to know, sir?" Her voice was soft, so soft he would not have heard her words had the distance between them been any greater.

"Wolf," he reminded her, once again tamping down the urge to reach for her, to take her in his arms and pull those decadent curves against him. "I ain't a *sir*. And I most certainly ain't a gentleman."

*Sir* felt as if it were an appellation that was better bestowed upon a lord. A lofty cove. A damned nob. And there was nothing proper or gentlemanly about Wolf. He was a Sutton, born to the rookeries. He would always be tarnished. A counterfeit, never the genuine article. Regardless of how much wealth he earned, no matter the respectability he fought to garner.

"I thought of you last night, alone in my bed."

Her words tore him from his ruminations, sending lust bolting through him. The confession was enough to unman him. Alone, in her bed? Had she touched herself? Brought herself to completion? The thought of her delicate fingers slicking through her silken quim, bringing herself to a writhing peak of pleasure, made his heart pound. Made him forget all the reasons he ought to leave this room—*hell, the entire establishment*—and never cross paths with his tempting Portia again.

Made him draw nearer to her when he should have gone.

Aye, she was the Siren, but it was too late. Wolf's ship had already been drawn onto the rocks.

Time to drown.

∼

What in heaven's name was she doing, taking such a reckless, foolish risk as pretending this man was her husband? And worse, she was lingering here with him, *flirting*. Making revelations better kept in the deepest, darkest secrets of the night. That she had thought of him alone in her bed. But it had been more than that, of course. Far more.

She had dreamt of him.

Of his hands on her body.

And to her shame, when she had awoken, it had been to the crashing wave of pleasure as her inner muscles contracted. She had reached her pinnacle while sleeping. Without ever having been touched.

Portia was not certain if it was because her body had gone so long without someone else's touch aside from her own and Wolf had reminded her what pleasure felt like, or if it was this man in particular who affected her so. This tall, broad-shouldered, callused-handed East End rogue who had kissed her breathless in his gaming hell.

Coming to Bellingham and Co. had been another rash decision. But after her brother's departure, remaining within the same four walls had been as loathsome a prospect as facing more of his wrath was. Edwin had been engaged with his tutor, and she had been unneeded, so she had covered the bruising on her cheek in the manner to which she had grown accustomed. Losing herself in some mindless distraction had seemed a boon.

Now, she was no longer certain.

Because there was far more danger for her here than there had been at Blakewell House. A different manner of danger, it was true. But danger nonetheless. If Granville were to hear word that she had been alone with Wolf at Bellingham and Co., pretending to be his wife, he would fly into another rage. And she was not certain he had yet recovered from the last.

She could not afford to anger him, because she could not afford to lose her son. Edwin was her beloved boy, the sole source of happiness in her existence.

"I'd be telling a fib if I were to say I didn't think of you last night too."

Wolf's low, delicious rasp stole her from her frenzied thoughts. He had thought of her? Warmth slid through her. She found herself moving toward him. Swaying.

He knew what she wanted, for he reached for her, his hands settling on her waist in a possessive hold that thrilled her in a primitive way. He was not rough or cruel. He may have claimed he was no gentleman, but he had shown her more tenderness than she had believed existed.

Her gloved hands settled on his shoulders, holding him to her, as she searched his gaze. *This is wrong, Portia. This is foolish. You must cease this nonsense at once.* The warnings she issued to herself tripped over themselves. But she could not seem to heed a single one. Because the heat and strength radiating from his big, masculine body was positively magnetic. And so was he.

"How?" she asked, a whisper.

The question was as forbidden as the answer. Wrong in every sense. She should not be here. Should not have gone to his gaming hell the night before, let alone allowed him to take such liberties. Just as she should not have returned his wicked kisses this afternoon.

"Naked," he said softly, his hungry stare dipping to her lips. "Naked in my bed."

She compressed her lips, attempting to maintain her composure, to tamp down the needy sound that longed to break free and further shame her. But she had been denied tenderness, gentleness, the kisses and caresses of a lover, for so very long. Her cold marriage had been no comfort to her in any sense save one, and whilst her son's welfare and happiness and future were of the utmost import to Portia, part of her long buried wondered why she could not also steal a small shred of happiness for herself.

She was a widow.

Blakewell was gone, and she had been a loyal and faithful wife to him for all the years of their marriage.

"I should not be here with you now, like this," she murmured, still reluctant to withdraw.

"You are free to leave," he reminded her, flexing the fingers on her waist that proved his hold was gentle.

She could escape with scarcely any effort. The problem was, she had no wish to make it. Absolutely no will to flee the circle of his arms. Her breasts were against his chest, and she felt the delicious hardness of that wall of muscle through the stiff boning of her stays. The pulsing between her thighs was insistent. The same desire that had overwhelmed her the day before in the surprisingly luxurious gaming hell office had beset her now, and she was helpless to resist.

Portia ran her tongue over her lips, a nervous gesture she could not seem to suppress. "You have managed to mire us in a situation from which there is no easy means of extrication."

She was blaming him because it was easier than admitting what she felt. Easier than surrendering. And because doing what she wanted was dangerous to everything she held dear. She had not been free to do as she wished in years. She ought to be accustomed to self-denial.

"Certainly there is." A slow, charming grin curved his lips. "You need only to move your feet, and they shall take you out the door."

The rogue. She had to bite her lip to stave off an answering smile. "You have informed that unwitting man we are husband and wife. Do you truly believe merely removing myself from this chamber will solve the problem you have created?"

"It doesn't feel like a problem at the moment." His head dipped, until his breath was fanning over her mouth in the prelude to a kiss that, just as he said, very much did *not* feel like a problem to Portia. "Not to me. Does it to you?"

Her hands—her silly, weak hands—appeared to have a mind of their own, for they were traveling now. Curling into the long, dark strands at his nape, where his hair brushed over his coat. Oh how she wished she were not wearing gloves, that she might experience the silken texture against her fingertips.

"No," she admitted, flustered by his proximity and her reaction both. "But that is, by very definition, a problem. I should not want to be here with you. Alone. Like this."

"I can't think of a better way for you to be. Than alone. With me. Like this." His grin deepened. "Or mayhap other ways."

It was the other ways, and his beautiful mouth, and his warmth and his strength and his hands and the devil-may-care attitude he espoused that were the true problem. For they were all, in sum, impossible to resist.

"He will be returning at any moment," she felt compelled to warn.

"Then we had best make the most of our time while we have it."

She thought of how they had made the most of their too-brief interlude the day before. Recalled his fingers skimming over her needy flesh. Her hems and petticoats pulled to her waist. The way he had taken command of her, knowing what she wanted before she had. How he had brought her to shuddering, delicious release.

Portia told herself to command her restraint. To step away. To forget all about this man. This Wolf.

But her brother was not here. And neither was anyone who could carry a tale to him. Not in this tidy little private room at Bellingham and Co. And the temptation to give in and allow herself a fleeting moment of passion and indulgence was so strong. Stronger than the last misguided urge that had set her life on the unhappy path she had thus far trod. Different in every way from what she had felt so long ago, as an immature girl who had been easily swayed by a handsome face. There was something deeper between herself and Wolf. A connection she had felt from the moment their gazes had met and held.

She had looked at him and *known* him. Known him in a way that made no sense and yet she could not ignore. She felt comfortable in his embrace. Protected, even. There was nothing that should make her feel this way. She scarcely knew him aside from their heated exchanges, frantic kisses, and his teasing smiles and easy charm.

"Being familiar with you is a very bad idea." She warned herself more than him. For she had much to lose.

*Everything.*

And he would return to his gaming hell, unaffected. No one could tear his life asunder. No one ruled over him with a damning fist.

"Tell me your name," he said again, brushing his lips over hers in the barest hint of a kiss.

Scarcely any touch at all, and yet the surge of longing that accompanied the sweep of his sinful mouth took her breath.

"It is better if you do not know it," she said, rubbing her lower lip along the seam of his. Unable to help herself. Unable to stop.

Because God, it felt good.

*Better* than good.

Wondrous, really.

And when was the last time she had allowed herself the

luxury of simply feeling? Of indulging in something for herself, purely for the pleasure of it? She had been nothing more than wife and mother for so long that she could not recall. The latter role meant everything to her. But this sudden glimpse of a life beyond the drudgery and duty she had known these last years, a reminder that she had once been carefree and wild, that she had been able to pursue her own happiness and pleasure, was nothing short of tantalizing.

"Then tell me when I can see you again. Stolen kisses in a frippery store ain't enough," he growled, one of his hands leaving her waist to cup her cheek.

Like her, Wolf was wearing gloves. And when his leather-clad thumb rubbed over the bruise she had concealed, she could not suppress her wince, for it was new and tender.

He went still, frowning at her. "What the devil happened here?"

The hot coals of humiliation stung her. He must have uncovered the careful handiwork she had used to hide the evidence of her brother's violence against her. Pear's Almond Bloom had ever stood her in faithful service, but no one had ever touched her face save Portia herself. And now, Wolf had seen the bruise.

"It is nothing," she lied hastily, accustomed to avoiding questions, mostly from her concerned lady's maid who had seen more contusions than Portia would have liked to admit since Blakewell's death and Granville's dominion over her life.

"It ain't nothing, Portia." His jaw was rigid, his countenance thunderous. "You're looking at a man who's been in his share of fisticuffs. I know the look of that mark. You've been struck. Slapped, I'd wager."

How was it that this stranger, whom she had only known

for the span of two days, had already seen and understood more of her than almost everyone in her inner circle?

"It is nothing," she repeated, for that was what it was.

She could not change the provisions of Blakewell's will. Nor could she remove herself from beneath her brother's thumb. Even in widowhood, she was trapped just as desperately and miserably as she had been in her marriage. The reminder was enough to make an icy chill of dread pass over her, chasing some of the ardor.

"Who hurt you?" he demanded, his voice curt and sharp.

The lash of anger in his tone was familiar but reassuring, for she knew that it was not directed at her. Rather, at Granville, where it belonged.

"No one." She slipped from his embrace. "I bumped my cheek on a piece of furniture quite accidentally. But now I truly must go. Lingering here with you is a foolish mistake."

Before he could offer further protest, she spun away from him, the stinging rush of shame bringing tears to her eyes, blurring her vision. Blindly, she fumbled for the latch on the door.

"Portia," he said, his voice strained. "Don't go."

But she had to.

The door opened, and she raced out, doing her best to pass through the haberdashery department without drawing undue attention to herself. The shopkeeper and his questions were not her concern. What she needed to do was put some necessary distance between herself and Wolf.

And hope she would never see him again.

As she rushed from the store into the drab world outside, a cold drizzle had begun to fall. It seemed a fitting accompaniment to the ice dwelling within her heart.

## CHAPTER 5

Portia Fairhaven, the Countess of Blakewell.
Wolf's mystery woman had a name.

A title as well, just as he had suspected.

And she also had some bastard in her life who had dared to raise his hand against her. A cowardly bully she was doing her utmost to protect. *Secrets.* He'd had damned well enough of those. His missing brother was filled with them, and now the one woman he could not shake free from his thoughts was doing everything in her power to keep them.

She'd made an error of judgment however, when she'd fled him at Bellingham and Co. Because he had followed her. After hastily making certain the carriage would continue awaiting Lily and that Sleepy Tom would escort her safely back to The Sinner's Palace, Wolf had hastily hired a hack and begun his pursuit.

His efforts had ultimately led him to where he was at this moment. Which was a rather precarious position indeed. Wolf was situated in the dark shadows of Lady Blakewell's library, watching the fire burn itself out in the grate as he lurked amongst the massive draperies adorning the mullioned windows. It had been a number of years since he had last gone about housebreaking, but like so many skills in life, once it was acquired, it was not easily forgotten. And so, he had stolen into the quiet of Blakewell House with relative ease, even for a man of his impressive size.

Aye, he thought with a rueful grin as he passed a hand over his jaw, his last attempt at playing *ken cracker*, as housebreakers were commonly known in the rookeries, had been as a much smaller lad. Stealing about the halls in the darkness was a damned sight easier when a cove wasn't large enough to nearly fill a bloody doorframe. However, he'd been pleased to discover his old trusted tools, the jemmy, roundabout, and screw which had always stood him in good stead were where he had left them when he had sworn he'd no longer dabble in the forbidden art of thievery.

As he waited for the familiar sounds of the household settling in for the night, he told his conscience he was not exactly breaking his promise to himself to forego housebreaking. After all, he had not found his way beneath Portia's roof—through a less-than-prohibitive door below stairs, as it happened—to steal from her. Rather, he had come to offer her his aid. The sight of the purple-red bruise marring her otherwise creamy cheek had filled him with protective fury. The urge to find the man who would so ill use her and give him the drubbing of the century had been strong.

But Portia had fled before he could offer her his help. And it was because he well understood she could be in some manner of danger, and that the bastard who had struck her and left his mark upon her silken skin could be in residence as well, that he had chosen to execute this rather unorthodox means of seeking an audience with her hours later.

His booted feet offered up a pang of irritation as he

continued his vigil at the window, prepared to bolt behind the voluminous tapestry if necessary. It should not be long now before he could make his escape and quietly climb the stairs leading to the private quarters. He could not afford for any of the servants to discover him and send for the watch. Wolf and his siblings had a number of charleys whose palms were kept slickly greased by Sutton coin to make certain the law did not interfere in their business. But no need to tempt fate and find himself cast into the hulks. No stirrings or footsteps had been heard for some time.

If he'd had a glim to cast light over his pocket watch, he might have known the time. A ticking mantel clock gave him the barest indication the hour was likely well past midnight. Early morning, and time for the last of the lingering servants to be abed so they might be rested for the next day's work. Thank Christ his brothers had not required his aid in watching the floor this evening at The Sinner's Palace.

His eyes were well-attuned to the low light flickering from the fireplace. Enough that when he decided to move at last, he was able to cross the sumptuous carpets unencumbered by the maze of heavy furniture scattered throughout the chamber. He had just reached the door with the intention he would seek Portia's chamber when a flickering glow beneath alerted him to the unexpected presence of another.

*Fuck!*

The vicious oath tore through his mind as Wolf searched frantically for a place where he could hide himself. There was nothing near enough—the blasted windows were on the opposite side of the chamber. The best he could manage was to hunker behind a damned chair, but even that would be—

The door opened, cutting his thoughts in half.

But the figure who entered the library, holding a lone candle aloft to illuminate the way, was not at all who Wolf had expected.

He released the breath he had not realized he had been holding as his gaze met that of a young lad's. The boy froze, eyes going wide as he took in what was undoubtedly the imposing height and size of a fully grown man he had not expected to be lurking in the library at this hour of the morning.

"Who are you, sir?" the lad asked, his voice giving away his fear with a slight hitch, which matched the tremble in his small hand as the candle bobbled.

A child.

He hadn't anticipated such an interruption.

Slowly, he stepped forward, then sank on his haunches so he and the boy were at eye level.

Wolf pressed a finger to his own lips, signaling for the lad to remain quiet. "I am a friend, lad. Not a foe. You needn't fear me."

The boy blinked, tilting his head to one side as he considered Wolf in the curious manner only a child could possess. "Why should I fear you?"

Why indeed?

It was apparent the youth before him had never been given cause to fret over housebreakers or other manner of criminals.

"You shouldn't," he repeated, keeping his voice as quiet and calm as possible. "I'm here as a guest."

That was a lie, but he hoped the lad was not clever enough to know the difference. All he needed was to suitably distract the boy and then find his way to Portia's chamber so that he could speak with her and determine what the bloody hell was happening. He needed to know why she had come to The Sinner's Palace, who had dared to strike her, and where he was going to hide that particular scoundrel's body.

But enough murderous thoughts for now. There was an innocent lad watching him with wide, attentive eyes.

"What manner of guest? I was not aware Mama had any guests in residence," he said. "When Aunt Jane comes up to Town, Mama always tells me."

*Mama.*

This lad was likely Portia's son, then. The resemblance was suddenly apparent to him, even in the glow of the lone candle. She was a widow, so of course she would have had children. The notion that she was a mother made an odd warmth creep into his chest. She had a child. Perhaps more than one, even. But it was this particular one, with hair the same color as hers and his solemn expression and glittering green eyes, that was currently Wolf's to distract.

He raised a brow. "Do I look like Aunt Jane to you, lad?"

The boy shook his head. "No, sir. You do not. Aunt Jane is a lady, for one thing. For another, she is not nearly as tall or as large and hairy."

Wolf nearly bit out a bark of laughter at the child's unfettered observation. He supposed it was true enough, though he fancied he had never before been referred to as *large and hairy*. He reckoned he *was* in need of a sound shave, but some whiskers on his jaw had never perturbed him. Indeed, it only served to make him appear more menacing to his foes. Also, he was dreadfully lazy in the morning, a shortcoming he willingly owned. Nights were when he came to life. They always had been. It was why remaining on the floor at The Sinner's Palace through the evening into the early hours of the morning had never proven a particular hardship for Wolf.

"It is fortunate indeed that your Aunt Jane and I do not bear any resemblance to one another," he managed.

"I should say," the lad agreed sagely. "Any lady with shoulders as broad as yours would do no credit to a dress."

Again, he had to fight the urge to chuckle. "Just so, lad.

Now then, suppose you might tell me what you are doing, slipping about the halls in the midst of the night. I don't imagine your mama would be happy to find you here."

The lad hung his head. "Please do not tell her, sir. She will be ever so vexed with me if she discovers I am not asleep, and she promised me honey cakes for breakfast if I was well-behaved today."

Wolf could not contain his smile. "Honey cakes for breakfast? I well understand the conundrum, lad. You have my promise I'll not tell her as long as you return to bed as you ought. It ain't done for a young shaver such as yourself to be wandering the halls at night. Christ, you're likely to set the curtains on fire."

"Mama says a gentleman never blasphemes," the lad informed him, frowning.

"Shite," he muttered.

"What does *shite* mean, sir?" inquired his inquisitive companion.

*Fucking hell.* He was certainly giving Portia's son an education, was he not? He ought to be more accustomed to watching his wayward tongue thanks to his older brother Jasper's twin daughters. Anne and Elizabeth were nearly of an age with the serious youth before him, he would guess, and whilst their upbringing with their mother had been less than genteel, Jasper's wife, Lady Octavia had threatened them all with a sound tongue lashing whenever any of them misspoke before the girls. He supposed her displeasure had something to do with the girls referring to one of Jasper's dogs as Arsehole...

But never mind that.

He cleared his throat. "That is not what I said at all, lad, and don't be repeating it again, to your mama or otherwise. What I said was I am *shy*."

And bloody stupid. How else to explain the fact that he had followed a woman who had run from him earlier that day, found his way into her house by nefarious means, and now was teaching her innocent son to swear?

The lad blinked. "I do not understand what being shy has to do with blaspheming."

*Absolutely nothing.*

He patted the boy on the shoulder. "You needn't fret over it. All you *do* need to do is return to your bed, where you belong."

"I am not tired. I thought to fetch a book."

Well, damn his eyes. None of this was proceeding as he'd hoped.

"But you just said you shan't be having your honey cakes in the morning if you don't obey your mama," he pointed out.

Admittedly, bargaining with small children was not one of his talents.

"She will not know if you do not tell her," the lad argued.

He could see Portia in the lad's stubborn intelligence. And there it was again, that odd warmth in his chest, sliding about. Making him feel things. Strange things.

*She has a son*, he reminded himself. *Perhaps you ought to go off and leave her alone as she wishes. Leave the lad to gallivant about the library as he would like. They ain't your concern.*

But then, thoughts of that bruise on her cheek returned. It was that, and the fear in her eyes as she had fled him earlier, which had brought him here. He could not lie; he wanted to know more about her because he was drawn to her. Drawn to her in a way he had not experienced in years. Mayhap never. But his desire for Portia was not what had ultimately brought Wolf to her home.

Had not brought him to break through her door using his old cracksman tools.

"I am duty and honor bound to tell your mother," he informed the lad sternly. "It would not be right to keep secrets from her."

She had secrets aplenty of her own.

"To do so would be a lie," he added for good measure. "And lying is a sin."

The lad hung his head once more before sending Wolf a sly look. "As is blaspheming."

Apparently, he had not fooled the cunning kiddy. A lad after his own heart, this one was.

Before Wolf could answer, the door to the library swung open once more, and a distinctly feminine figure stepped over the threshold, holding a blazing brace of candles high. The lovely, familiar planes of Portia's high cheekbones were illumed. Even in shadows and the low glow of simple candlelight, she made his heart pound and heat unfurl in his belly. Caught as he was, he allowed himself to devour the sight of her, clad in a prim dressing gown buttoned up to the throat, her hair unbound around her shoulders in dark, exquisite waves, and the tease of her bare feet beneath the hem of her gown. There was a strange intimacy to the moment, to his presence here, that made the breath freeze in Wolf's lungs.

"Edwin, how many times have I told you that it is forbidden to sneak into the library at night when—" Her words ended on a gasp as she pressed a hand to her heart, eyes wide. "Wolf!"

~

PORTIA WILLED her rapidly thudding heart to slow, holding a hand there to stave off the abject fear which had initially sliced through her when she had realized her son was not alone in the library. That the shadowy figure of a very large man was hunched down before him. When she had lifted the brace of candles and his gaze had jerked to hers, the immediate terror fled, recognition taking its place. Along with a warm, reassuring wave of familiarity.

*Relief.*

But then she recalled just as swiftly that there was only one manner in which the man who had kissed her breathless on more occasions than she would prefer to admit could have found himself standing in her library at midnight. Speaking to Edwin as if he infiltrated the libraries of people he scarcely knew as a common event.

"What are you doing here?" she demanded.

He rose slowly to his full, impressive height, and she inwardly admonished herself not to admire the breadth of his shoulders. She failed miserably, however. It had been mere hours since she had seen him last, and yet her gaze drank in every part of him as if she had been starved for the sight of that tall form, his finely molded lips, and that hazel stare that made her feel as if she were ablaze.

"I am your guest, my lady." He nodded his head toward her son, as if she required reminding they had an audience, and then he swept into the most elegant bow she had ever witnessed a housebreaker perform.

Not that she had ever seen a housebreaker before.

But she imagined most of them did not bow to the occupants of their home with such flawless masculine grace. Or kiss with such seductive tenderness. Her heart was pounding anew, but not with fear this time. Rather, with the effect of his nearness.

He was here.

In her home.

Her library.

With her son.

Oh, the damage that could be done, should any of the

servants learn there was a strange man beneath her roof at midnight. She had made some discreet inquiries with her butler, lady's maid, and housekeeper this evening. However, she had still yet to discover who was the source of Granville's information. She would not be spied upon in her own home, that she had vowed.

"You are my most unexpected guest," she told Wolf through gritted teeth.

Part of her was thrilled he had come to her, finding his way inside through means she was certain had been positively criminal. However, the rest of her, the motherly instincts that had driven her steadily through all the unhappy choices she had been forced to make in her life, told her she must not allow herself to bask in his presence. She would need to send him on his way with all haste.

First, though, came the matter of Edwin. She had no wish for her son to become involved in her brother's machinations. And she had no doubt that Edwin may, in his unknowing eagerness to impress the uncle he did not know was so dastardly, reveal Wolf's nighttime presence here to Granville. She would need to proceed with caution. They both would.

Wolf sent her a knowing half grin that sent another unwanted rush of heat over her. "Ain't unexpected guests the most interesting sort?"

When they looked and kissed as he did, yes. However, she could not very well give such an imprudent response, and not with her son as innocent witness.

"May I still have honey cakes tomorrow for breakfast, Mama?" interjected Edwin in a pleading tone that never failed to pierce her heart. "I only came to the library to find the Latin treatise Mr. Leslie spoke of during today's lessons."

She knew her son. He was intelligent and clever, but he

most certainly did *not* enjoy reading Latin, and nor was he particularly adept at motivating himself to purse his studies. The latest report from his tutor, Mr. Leslie, had been a rather grim assessment of Edwin's knowledge of Latin declension.

"Edwin," she began gently, "are you telling me one of your tales?"

Her son shook his head, eyes wide. "Never, Mama."

"Tales," Wolf muttered. "That a lady's way of saying a lad is telling a fib?"

She shot him a quelling glance. "It is none of your concern, sir."

"Suppose not." He shrugged, then crossed his arms over his not inconsiderable chest.

The man could have been hewn from granite. Indeed, in the flickering shadows, he appeared to possess the stature of a Greek god rather than a mere mortal man. He was all strength and lean muscle, tall and wide and overwhelming.

And handsome, too.

*Cease thinking about how beautiful Wolf is*, she cautioned herself, jerking her gaze back to her son.

"Edwin," she tried again, "were you truly looking for a volume of Latin, or did you sneak into the library to work on your drawing again?"

Her son, while not naturally adept at the studies expected of him and other young lords, was a particularly gifted artist. Portia kept his pastel crayons and paper supply in the library, and she had already caught him on a separate occasion sneaking out of the nursery after he should have long since been to bed for the night. An unexpected advancement in one of his pictures had led her to believe he had been stealing away when he was not supervised by his tutor or herself. Ever since, she had taken to making one last pass of the library and halls before retiring in truth for the evening.

Her son bit his lip, and she could almost hear his mind

frantically working to form a suitable excuse that would allow him his morning allotment of honey cakes.

"Edwin," she prodded, uncomfortably aware of Wolf's gaze on her.

It was like the heat from a fire, the effect of his stare. Like the touch of a lover on her skin. Her cheeks went hot. But still, her son did not save her by offering up a response. Instead, he shuffled his small feet on the carpets, looking torn between admitting the truth or attempting a lie to see if he might achieve the reward of his sweet breakfast treat after all.

"Lad," Wolf intoned. "Are you certain you are telling your mother the truth?"

Her astonished gaze flew to him. He shrugged, then offered her a small smile. The words were on her tongue, crowding it, the admonishment he so rightly deserved. How dare he presume to interfere in the dialogue between herself and her son? He did not belong here, in this room, beneath this roof, in her life. And yet he believed that his intervention in the matter would inspire Edwin to admit he was lying?

It was absurd.

It was maddening!

It was—

"No, sir," Edwin conceded, head hanging. "I am not telling Mama the truth." His head shot up, his expression wary, looking as if he were about to burst into tears. "Have I disappointed you, Mama? I am sorry. I only wanted to complete my dragon's tail, and then I would have gone to bed as you asked."

Portia stared dumbly at her son. He had confessed the truth to a stranger, when he had been reluctant to admit it to her, his *mother*. She was at once pleased Wolf had been able to gently and easily coerce her son into the admission and resentful she had not been the one to do so herself. Yet another of her failings.

One in a litany of them.

"Edwin," she managed to scold, giving him her most disappointed expression. "Lying is wrong, and so is leaving the nursery when are you to be abed for the night, getting your rest."

"I am sorry, Mama," he said, and promptly dissolved into a fit of weeping.

But it was the sort of sobbing where he valiantly tried to suppress his tears like the somber little lord he had been told he ought to be. Her heart ached. She gathered him in her arms and held him tight, relishing the feeling of his small, vibrant body next to hers, and buried her face in his hair, inhaling the familiar, beloved scent.

"Do not cry, darling," she told him. "I am not angry with you. However, I will have your promise you shall not wander about so late in the night again."

"I promise," he sniffled.

Ever aware of Wolf's gaze on her, watching, she lifted her head to meet the intensity of his hazel stare. The unguarded expression on his handsome face took her by surprise.

Tenderness, or so she thought. And longing too. Her heart gave an answering pang, and she knew that she was wading into dangerous waters indeed.

"Come then," she told her son, "let us get you back to bed where you belong. Sir, if you would kindly escort yourself to where you belong as well?"

The last, she directed to Wolf.

He nodded. "Aye. I'll do that, then."

She licked her lips, wishing she could say more, wishing she could reach for him. Touch him one more time. But knowing she did not dare.

"Good evening," she told him, and then turned with her

arm around her son's thin shoulders, guiding him from the library.

She swore she felt the heat of Wolf's hungry stare on her as she went. But she did not turn back, not even for one last glance.

It was for the best.

## CHAPTER 6

She'd told Wolf to return to where he belonged.

So naturally, he'd found his way to the chamber that was hers. It hadn't been difficult. With the rest of the busy household abed, he had slipped through the halls with ease, familiar enough with the layout of town houses thanks to his various forays within them—as a guest both invited and uninvited. He had opened two doors to chambers which were clearly not in use. On the third, he had found hers.

A fire in the grate was his first indication.

The second was the scent—elegant and complex, like a bouquet of flowers, clean and bright and beautiful. Maudlin though the sentiment was, Wolf could not shake it from his mind. And the third was the obvious feminine presence. The pictures on the walls, a vase of fresh hothouse blooms on a table, a stack of well-read books by the bed, the extravagant counterpane and intricate paper-hangings with an assortment of vibrant birds and flowers.

Hands clasped behind his back, Wolf paced the room, waiting for her to return from the nursery. Portia had assumed he would see himself out by the same means he had entered and leave her secrets intact. But the sight of her bruised cheek, hidden adroitly by some manner of cosmetic, remained burned into his mind. He could not forget it any more than he could forget her. Someone had hurt her, and he damn well wanted to know who and why.

At last, the door to her chamber opened, and Portia stepped inside, the brace of candles still in hand, casting a warm glow over the space and chasing the shadows. She gasped when she saw him, the portal falling softly closed at her back.

"What are you doing in my chamber?" she demanded, her voice quiet yet loud enough to carry and bearing the lash of her disapproval.

He strode forward. "You said I was to escort myself to where I belonged."

He stopped when he was near enough to touch her but restrained himself. His attempt to tease did not win a smile from her as he had hoped. She eyed him nervously, her countenance pale. It occurred to him that she had reapplied whatever paint she had used to hide the bruise, for it was currently not visible once again.

"To your gaming hell," she countered crisply. "That is where I intended for you to go, or to wherever it is that you lay your head at night. Your mistress, perhaps?"

He did not think he misunderstood her last question. She wanted to know more about him. To be certain there was not another woman in his life. She was in luck. There were none. Had been none for some time. Not for a lack of trying from some morts. He just hadn't been interested.

He shook his head slowly. "I haven't a mistress, Portia."

"Oh." She nodded, lips compressed. "Yes. Good."

"I would never have kissed you if I were otherwise entangled," he felt compelled to tell her.

Why, he knew not. He expected it was because he was

touched in the head. Certainly, he owed the Countess of Blakewell no explanation of how he lived his life or with whom he shared his bed.

Portia placed the brace of candles upon a nearby table. "You cannot be here."

He made an expansive gesture, as if he were presenting something triumphantly. "I can indeed, my lady, for here I am."

She caught her lower lip between her teeth, as if attempting to subdue a chuckle. "You are deliberately misunderstanding me, just as you did when I told you to leave."

She needed him, and he was not going to bloody well abandon her. Not when he knew someone was ill using her. Not when she had an innocent lad beneath her roof.

Wolf passed a hand along his jaw. "You never told me to leave, Countess. If you had, I'd have gone. You told me to go where I belonged. I reckon I belong here as well as anywhere else."

Aye, he belonged where she was. He felt it to his marrow. Two days he had known her. But the time did not matter. There was something incontestably deep and true between them. A bond which spoke to him. And he was a cove who very much did not wish for a woman in his life. Especially not one who was so far out of reach.

"You are in my bedchamber," she said.

As if he needed her to tell him they were standing in her private space, a bed looming on the wall opposite, invitingly empty and beckoning. But that was not what he had come here for, even if he had spent the previous night haunted by thoughts of her naked in his arms. He had come here to help her, damn it.

"It seemed a plummy place for us to talk about that bruise on your cheek and who gave it to you," he said, his gaze dipping to the spot where he knew violence secretly marred her skin.

How could anyone have raised his hand to any woman? Only a cowardly, vicious, heartless bastard would do so. And Wolf was going to do everything in his power to make certain the whoreson never raised a hand to hurt Portia again.

"I already told you nothing happened and it is none of your concern," she said coolly. "Now, if you please, go. You cannot linger here. If anyone should discover your presence..."

Her words trailed off, but he did not mistake the tone of fear lacing them.

"You are a widow, and this is your household, is it not?" he probed. "Surely you would not be the only society lady to take a lover."

Indeed, he knew she would not be. The peccadilloes of the quality were notorious. Many an unhappy wife had found contentedness in the arms of another, and vice versa. *Floating hell*, the gossip that swirled at the tables of The Sinner's Palace, when men's tongues had been loosened by liquor, were enough to shock even the most jaded of rakehells.

Her lips parted, as if she were searching for words but unable to find them. After a pause, she spoke. "You are not my lover."

*Yet*, he wanted to add.

He could not say what it was about the Countess of Blakewell that made him want to abandon every guiding principle that had ruled his life since Lydia. But regardless of the reasons, he wanted Portia. He somehow knew she was meant to be in his arms, in his bed. And he was meant to be in hers. He understood it in an elemental sense, and he had a suspicion she did as well.

"Since we are not lovers, then there is no need to fear gossip over my presence here," he argued smoothly. "I am a friend, come to offer my aid."

"Friends do not kiss their friends the way you kissed me."

He smiled. "No, I suppose they do not. But why do you not tell me who it is you fear? The servants in your house? A male relative?"

Her eyes widened slightly at the last, and he knew he had not missed his guess.

"No one," she stubbornly denied.

Wolf remained unconvinced. "Then why do you hide the bruising on your cheek?"

Her gaze flicked to a point over his shoulder. "Because I am vain."

Like her son, she was a dreadful liar.

"I want to help you, Portia."

Her emerald eyes returned to his. "I do not want your pity."

Ah, he had wounded her pride. He was going about this all wrong, it would seem. But curse it, he would not simply walk away from her. Not like this.

"It ain't my pity you've got, woman," he countered, surrendering to the impulse to touch her.

He moved slowly, carefully, as if she were a wild creature he feared might take sudden flight. If he had known she had been ill-treated by another earlier in the day, at Bellingham and Co., he never would have been so forward with her. Would not have silenced her with that kiss. And he regretted his bold actions now. With delicate care, he cupped her cheek, the one that was neither injured nor hidden beneath a fine layer of cosmetic. His thumb swept over her cheekbone, relishing the smooth caress of her skin on his, unencumbered by gloves.

Her hand came up to his, not to pry his touch away as he

had feared, but to hold him there. "What is it, then?" she asked softly, her low voice almost a whisper.

"Ain't it plain to see?" he asked gruffly, for it had been a long time—years—since he had last allowed himself to be vulnerable to a woman.

He felt rusty and raw. He was not a petticoats chaser as his brother Jasper had been before falling in love and marrying. He was not a charmer as his brother Rafe was. And he was not a rakehell as his brother Hart had been, either. As for his brother Loge... *Hell*, Wolf did not even know his brother now. He wondered if he ever had. Regardless, he was not accustomed to wooing and winning the fairer sex.

She sighed, those long lashes of hers drifting closed and shielding her thoughts for a moment as she swayed toward him. "Nothing is plain to me any longer."

The admission seemed as if it were torn from her.

A revelation she had tried to keep to herself and yet had nonetheless conceded. The sudden, primitive need to protect her seized Wolf with such ferocity, it surprised him.

"Tell me who did this to you, Countess," he urged gently. Tenderly. "I'll make certain he can never hurt you again."

She shook her head, pressing her lush lips together, her eyes opening. The sorrow in their mossy depths hit him like a fist to the gut. "You cannot make certain of that. No one can."

*Blast.*

"Let me."

"There is nothing you can do about my plight." She sent him a tremulous smile. "I am quite trapped. My husband's will has ensured it."

*Christ.* The earl must have been a bastard, to leave his widow in the hands of a monster who would strike her.

"Tell me his name, and I'll give him a basting he'll never forget," he vowed harshly.

"Doing so would only create more problems for the both of us." Her dulcet voice was as sad as her countenance.

If he had not known better, he would swear he had imagined the passionate woman who had so boldly kissed him the day before. The one who had seized her desires freely and without shame, as was her right. But that had been before someone had struck her.

He clenched his jaw. "Aye, I understand. I'm not aiming to cause more problems for you, but to protect you from 'arm."

There went his polish and all the efforts of the tutoring Jasper had commissioned to erase the East End from his speech. In moments of fury and intense emotion, it remained. As telltale as the calluses on his hands.

"No one can protect me," she said. "I find myself in this position because of the decisions I made, and the burden is mine alone to bear."

He didn't like her calm acceptance of what was surely an untenable situation. Fury rose on her behalf.

He stroked her cheek. "Being beaten ain't a burden, Portia. It's a sin."

Her eyes glittered with unshed tears. "You scarcely even know me. Why should you care?"

Why, indeed? The answer was obvious. He shouldn't care. She was right; he had only known her the span of two days. *Floating hell*, he had only discovered her full name after following her here to her fancy town house. But he could not explain it, not to himself and certainly not to Portia. He felt inexplicably tied to her. Those heated kisses they had shared proved the attraction was there, burning with an undeniable flame. But there was also something more. Something deeper.

"You came to The Sinner's Palace for a reason, no?" he asked instead of answering her query.

She blinked, stubborn tears clinging to her lashes, one

sliding down her cheek for him to catch with his thumb. "You need not concern yourself with that, either."

"I'm aiming to help you," he countered sternly. "That's why I'm here."

Well, that and the fact he couldn't seem to get enough of her. But it was not lust governing him now, propelling him on this path. It was a far less transitory emotion.

"I do not even know your surname."

"Sutton," he said. "There you are, then. It's settled. I've given you my name in exchange for another. Tell me who hit you, and I'll thrash the devil to within an inch of his life."

She shook her head. "No thrashing."

"He deserves it," he growled, vexed that she continued to conceal the identity of whomever it was who had dared to strike her. "But if you'll not surrender his name, then perhaps you'll tell me why you came to The Sinner's Palace yesterday."

She had not come to kiss him. That much he knew. He was damned glad she had, however.

"I was searching for someone."

"Who?" he asked.

A lover? He hoped not.

"My brother." Her countenance became troubled. "His mother led me to believe he was perhaps working at your establishment."

That gave him pause. "A brother of yours?"

Seemed deuced unlikely.

She sniffed, reminding him she had been doing her utmost to suppress her tears. "A half brother, in truth. Avery is illegitimate."

*Ah.* Suddenly, he understood her reticence.

Wolf released her cheek before reaching into his coat to extract a handkerchief, offering it to her. "Take this, love."

She accepted the square of linen, biting her lower lip. "Thank you."

Portia dabbed at her eyes and cheeks.

"Was it the bastard brother who did this to you?" he asked, thinking that when he found this Avery, whomever he was, Wolf was going to show him why striking a defenseless lady was a bleeding bad idea.

"No," she said quietly. "I haven't found Avery. My intentions yesterday were…well, I was led astray."

Aye, he well recalled how led astray they'd *both* been. The seductive wet heat of her on his fingers would haunt him until his last breath.

"And then someone discovered where you had gone and what you had done and took out his anger on you?" he guessed, wishing he knew why she was so determined to protect her abuser.

Her fingers tightened on the handkerchief as she extended it toward him. "Thank you, Mr. Sutton."

*Bloody hell*, he was in her chamber. He had stroked her quim the day before. He was not a bloody stranger.

"Wolf," he corrected, "and keep the handkerchief."

He fancied the notion of her having something of his, he would not lie. But he would be damned if he would admit that aloud. His response to this woman—the way she made him feel—was unprecedented.

"Thank you," she said. "But you should go. You have tarried here long enough, and with each moment you remain, the risk of discovery heightens."

She was fearful in her own household. Distrustful of her servants. Someone held a great deal of power over the Countess of Blakewell, and since the earl was dead, it had to be someone else close enough to want to control her.

"Your father?" he guessed.

Because while a patriarch was meant to protect and care

for his family, no one knew better than Wolf what an utter louse a father could be. His own had been lower than low.

"My father is dead."

As was his. No one was sad about it.

"An uncle, then? Another brother?" he continued to guess.

Her response—parted lips, a sudden pallor in her otherwise healthy complexion—told him everything he needed to know.

"Wolf," she protested.

If she refused to tell him, he would find out in his own way. He had men in his employ and money in his purse. He'd discover who it was she feared, and he'd do everything in his power to make certain the bastard could never hurt her again.

He studied her. "You needn't answer. I can tell I'm not far from the mark. When can I see you again?"

Her countenance was stricken. "You cannot. I should never have... What happened between us must not happen again. I have a son, whose needs I must place before my own."

Fair enough. He would never presume to come between a mother and her child. But what if whomever it was who had struck her decided to take out his wrath on the lad? Part of him knew this was not his battle to wage. That what happened to Portia and her son was none of his concern. Yet, he could not simply forget he had ever met her.

"But what are your needs?" he asked, reminded once more that they were alone, in her chamber, and she was clad in nothing more than that temptingly prim dressing gown and likely an equally proper night rail beneath.

The prospect of peeling her out of both should not have been so appealing.

Especially not when romantic entanglements would not serve either of them well. He did not need a woman in his bed; he never had. And she did not need more trouble, as she had rightly perceived he could bring her.

And still…

Still, he could not simply walk away from her.

Instead, he waited in the intimate shadows of her chamber, surrounded by her scent, and awaited her answer.

∽

NEEDS.

He wanted to know her *needs*.

*Tell him you have none. Demand that he leave. Go to sleep.*

Yes, that was what she should do. She *should* tell Wolf Sutton to leave her alone. Make him promise to never again seek her out. But she had been doing what she should ever since she had found herself unwed and carrying the child of a man she'd wrongly believed had loved her. To protect her son, she had married a man thirty years her senior. She had become the Countess of Blakewell. She had lived a life above reproach. Nary a hint of scandal or passion. She had spent all these years doing what she should rather than what she wanted. Had tamped down her every need. Ignored the part of her that longed for something more.

For what she had felt yesterday and then again earlier today in this man's arms.

It was dangerous.

Reckless.

Foolish.

"You should go," she repeated, reminding him as much as warning herself.

But even as she issued the words, she was moving. Taking one step forward. Then another. Bridging the distance between them until he was near enough to touch again. And touching him proved impossible to resist. She tucked the handkerchief into a pocket she had sewn into her dressing gown and then flattened her palms on his chest.

His heat and strength were enough to make a burst of longing rush over her.

"You want me to leave?" he asked, standing still.

Neither taking her in his arms as she craved nor moving away.

She should say yes.

But there was something so very tempting about Mr. Wolf Sutton. Perhaps it was his impressive height, his broad shoulders. Or his wickedly handsome face. His tenderness. The kindness he had shown Edwin earlier. The disparity between their stations. The way he kissed her.

*Good heavens*, mayhap it was all those things combined.

Whatever the reason, she could not deny him, and she could not resist him. And in this moment of incredible weakness, him here with her, she did not want to. *He is here*, whispered a dark, forbidden part of herself she had thought long ago walled off. *No one has seen him sneak into your chamber. Why not take advantage of the night? Why not give in to what you want?*

And what she wanted was him. *Wolf.* More of his greedy kisses and tender caresses. More of his touch on her, those rough hands bringing her such pleasure.

"No," she whispered, her gaze falling to his lips. "I don't want you to leave." She paused, swallowing against a rush of old shame and fear, the kind that had been haunting her for so long. "I want you to stay."

For the next minute.

For the next hour.

For the night.

Whatever it entailed, she was fast losing her grip on the reins of her control.

He eyed her solemnly, his hands at last settling on her

waist, anchoring her body to his in a way that felt at once familiar and right. "It ain't my intention to cause you trouble. I'll be discreet."

*Discreet.*

That was a word often used by lovers. Aside from Landringham, she had never had one. After the viscount's betrayal, she had never wanted another, had never even thought about opening her heart and body again.

Was that what she was intending? Was that what this—inviting Wolf to remain, touching him—meant? And why did the possibility that it was leave her breathless?

"You must go before the servants are about," she said, taking the leap.

*There.* She had just invited him into her bed. Had just asked him to be her lover.

Just for one night, she thought wildly. What was the harm? Why not take what she wanted? Why could this man not be hers for just a sliver of time? Her heart was suddenly galloping, and she was about to change her mind when he leaned his forehead to hers.

"Tell me what you want." He ran the blade of his nose against hers in a gentle caress.

*Everything.* The world suddenly seemed alive with possibility, like the sun rising bright and true to preside over a new day.

Her hands slid up his chest, detesting the layers of civility keeping her from him. She slipped her fingers beneath his waistcoat, nothing but his shirt separating her bare skin from his. He was so warm, the thumping of his heart against her splayed palm proving he was as affected as she was.

"I...I don't know what I want," she confided. "It has been so very long for me..."

It had been years. But would that scare away a man like Wolf? Did he suppose her to be experienced? Did he think her the sort of jaded society wife who had taken more lovers than she could count? Was that what he wanted? Was that why he had come to her here, at her town house?

"It has been a lifetime for me," he said then, his voice quiet yet firm as he rubbed his cheek against hers.

For a brief moment, the abrasion of his whiskers on her skin delighted her to the point of distraction. Her nipples hardened into demanding buds beneath her night rail. Gradually, however, his words stole through the haze of lust that had enveloped her susceptible mind.

A lifetime for him.

Meaning he had never made love to a woman before?

Her head jerked back and she searched his hazel gaze, trying to determine whether or not she had heard him correctly. "A lifetime?"

"Aye." He sent her a crooked grin that melted something inside the icy confines of her heart. "I've never bedded a woman before."

He had *never*? Surprise mingled with another, foreign emotion. She would have believed a man of his innate charm and self-assured nature to be a seasoned rakehell. That he would have had half the ladies of London ready to throw themselves at him at the slightest provocation. Indeed, he likely had. But he had clearly not wished to indulge.

Portia blinked. "But you want to. With me."

The words emerged as a statement. But she intended them as a question. Portia was hopelessly flustered, both from his revelation and her reaction to him. She did not recall ever desiring anyone as much as she longed for Wolf. It made no sense, for she scarcely knew him.

"I want to stay here with you for a bit of time." He kissed her cheek. "If you'll have me. I promise I'll be gone before anyone should know I've been here, save you and the lad."

Her fingers answered for her, hungrily sliding up his

chest to the simple knot of his cravat. She fumbled with it for just a moment before the cloth came loose. "Yes."

He hadn't said what he wanted, what he expected, whether or not he intended to make love to her. Not precisely. And perhaps it didn't matter. She wanted him here. *Needed* him here. Whatever part of himself he gave her, she would accept. No man had ever made her feel so protected, so cherished, in the manner Wolf possessed.

And after the unpleasantness of her brother's call earlier that day and the violence which had been visited upon her, there was something so very comforting in finding herself in a protective embrace. In being desired. But not just by anyone.

By Wolf.

He dragged his lips along her jaw in slow, hot kisses that she felt to her toes. He savored her—there was no other way to describe the painstaking, sensual torture of his mouth gliding over her skin. When his mouth dipped, settling into her throat above the collar of her dressing gown, she allowed her head to fall back, giving him more of her eager flesh.

He sucked on her skin, and her knees went weak. Fortunately, he was prepared, for his arms banded around her waist to keep her from crumpling to the floor. Her desperate fingers sought the silken waves of his hair, threading through the dark strands. How good he felt, against her, surrounding her. So strong and yet tender. He caught the lobe of her ear in his teeth and gently tugged, the unexpected action causing a corresponding throb in her cunny.

He guided them both toward her bed as he tongued the hollow behind her ear, a place she had never dreamed would elicit flames of need skipping up and down her spine, making her shiver and writhe in his arms, seeking to get closer still. But he denied her what she longed for, instead urging her to seat herself on the edge of the bed. She did as he wanted, reluctantly separating her aching body from his. And then, his clever hands had moved from her waist to the buttons lining her dressing gown. One by one, he plucked, his gaze following the progress of his movement, his countenance stormy.

The last button slid from its mooring, and he peeled her sleeves down her arms, helping her to shed the shielding garment. She shivered when his gaze found her pebbled nipples, poking through the fine linen of her simple night rail.

He cupped her breast, rubbing his thumb over the aching tip. "Beautiful."

His praise made her *feel* beautiful. Portia arched into his hand as he caressed her with agonizing leisure, as if they had all night to devour each other and a hundred more nights after this. But they did not. All they had was this one. She had reconciled herself to that fact. If Granville discovered she had a lover, he would take Edwin from her care. There was no doubt. And she could not risk the loss of her precious son.

"Will you take this off?" he asked quietly, his hungry stare burning into hers as he caught the fabric of her night rail between his thumb and forefinger. "I want to see you."

She was suddenly painfully aware of all the parts of her body she had failed to consider, first as a wife and later as a widow. The much fuller curves of her hips, the larger waist and full bottom. When she had been a debutante, she had been thin as a reed. But when she had been heavy with child, her body had altered, and the changes which had been wrought had never entirely been undone. She had not shown herself to a man—entirely nude—ever. Not even Landringham.

But she would not think of him now. Her son's father was a coldhearted scoundrel who had bedded her until her love had become an inconvenience, and she had no wish to compare the furtive couplings they had shared to what she was experiencing now with Wolf.

As if reading her thoughts, Wolf kissed her shoulder, then her breast. "You needn't be shy with me, love. But if you'll be wanting to leave it on, I understand."

How compassionate he was. She had never expected to find a man of such mysterious depths when she had summoned her bravado and marched into The Sinner's Palace.

"I want to see you first," she said.

The grin he gave her melted more of that stern ice she had thought impenetrable.

*This night is all we shall have.*

She tamped down a painful surge of disappointment at the reminder.

Any lingering disagreeable feelings were promptly dashed away as Wolf went to work on removing his coat and waistcoat. They fell to the floor in a sinful whisper of sound, leaving him looming over her in nothing more than his shirt and trousers. But once he had begun his task, Wolf proved determined. With the hasty flick of his long fingers, three buttons came undone, and then he caught the white fabric in his fists and hauled it over his head, revealing the mouthwatering expanse of his upper body to her feasting gaze.

His belly was taut, all lean, corded muscle. And his chest was broad, a sprinkling of dark hair adorning it, along with something else that drew her interest. It appeared as if it were a drawing made in ink, etched into his skin.

Portia leaned forward, her hand stealing out to touch him of its own accord as she marveled at the inking of a dragon with its wings unfurled, as if in flight. Her fingers traced over the tail, which curled below his nipple. The heat of his skin, along with the light dusting of chest hair, pleased her fingertips, bringing the flames inside her even higher.

"You have a tattoo," she said, a silly observation because surely he knew what was upon his own body.

And what a lovely body it was.

"I forgot about her," he said ruefully, glancing down at his chest. "I've had her for a few years." Idly, he rubbed the dragon's head and wings. "Hopefully I ain't too frightening."

"Frightening? Heavens, no." Intrigued, she traced over the dragon, following the dark curves from her tail, back to her wings. "You are beautiful."

The urge to feel him beneath her lips rose, and before she could deny herself, she pressed her mouth to his lean belly, kissing him there, feeling the skin contract, his muscles tense beneath her.

"This old hide of mine ain't beautiful," he rasped, relinquishing the dragon painted on his chest in favor of sifting his hands through her hair. "Now this—*you*—are true beauty, Countess."

Strangely, when he called her by her title, she did not find it as loathsome as she once had. But then, to others, she had always been Lady Blakewell. Few had ever called her Countess. And in his deep, melodic voice it sounded like a term of endearment. Highest praise.

She was suddenly glad she had unbound her hair and been brushing it out when she had thought she heard a telltale creak in the halls before conducting her final evening's pass through the house, and had gone to investigate. The glide of Wolf's fingers through her long hair was nothing short of luxurious. She kissed his belly again to show him her enjoyment, and inhaled the musky, male scent of him. Her mouth traveled lower as his fingers grazed her scalp in delicious ministrations. She bowed her head and followed the dark trail of hair that led to the waistband of his trousers. The thick length of him stood in proud relief against the falls, and she cupped him in her palm, gratified when he groaned and jerked his hips, filling her hand with his rigid cock.

He wanted her.

How pleased the knowledge made her feel.

Pleased and proud and not just a little wicked. A great deal wicked. Powerful, too. She stroked him through his trousers, and he caught a handful of her hair, tugging her head back with gentle insistence so their gazes met and held.

"Christ, woman. You make me want to break every vow I've ever made."

His low, husky confession also pleased her. She stroked again, grasping him as best as she could manage through the fabric separating her from what she wanted. Her only other lover had been far more experienced than she. A rake who had masterfully wooed her and persuaded her to give him everything he had wanted. She liked that Wolf was the opposite. Not a jaded libertine but a man who had somehow, impossibly, chosen her alone.

But this was not enough. Now that she had him half-naked and hard, her hands on him, and his on her, she had to have more. Because this was her last chance. Had to be her last chance. Tonight's folly could never again be repeated.

"I want you in my mouth," she whispered, still holding his stare.

He clenched his jaw. "You don't need to do that, love. That ain't why I stayed."

She knew he had not remained with expectations of her instinctively, just the way she knew this man would never raise a hand to her. He would never hurt her. Though his size far surpassed Granville's, there was nothing to fear from Wolf. Neither his East End roots nor his name nor the dragon emblazoned on his chest shook her. She wanted to bring him pleasure. Wanted to forget, for these few, stolen hours, that her life was not her own and this man could never be hers.

"Has a woman ever done that for you before?" she dared to ask, for while he had never shared a woman's bed, it was entirely possible he had some experience. His skilled touches and smoldering kisses certainly suggested so.

She could not resist caressing his cock again, loving the heat and the thickness of him against her palm. Her inner muscles clenched as she imagined what it would feel like to have him inside her.

"Fucking hell," he muttered, a flush staining his cheekbones. "No."

It was wrong, she knew, the shiver of lust his admission sent through her. "May I?"

"Countess…"

Her title ended on a hiss as she slid a button free. He was not wearing smalls beneath, and it was a much-appreciated discovery. One more button, and he sprang free, thick and long and more beautiful than she had imagined. She took him in hand, reveling in the velvet heat as she stroked.

"You'll unman me, if you carry on like that," he ground out, his hand clasping hers and staying her motions.

The thought that her mere touch had such an effect on him was heady indeed. "Tell me what you want."

# CHAPTER 7

"You." The lone word was torn from Wolf.

Her soft hand was wrapped around his cock, and he was aching to be inside her. He had not been lying when he had said she tempted him to forget his vows. Nothing seemed more important than making love to her. Not the past, nor the present. Certainly not the future.

"Then have me," she said, and never had there been an invitation he had wanted more.

He cupped her cheek and kissed her, taking her mouth with his. Her lips were full and soft and warm, and they clung to his so sweetly. He did not dare linger too long for fear of losing his head.

Instead, he kissed a path to her ear. "Let's take off your night rail, love."

He released his hold on her and straightened. Although he mourned the loss of her touch on his aching cock, the sight of her creamy legs being revealed to him as she raised the hem of her gown to her waist was more than enough compensation. Christ, but she was lovely. All feminine curves and lush skin. She shifted slightly, dislodging the skirt from beneath her rump, and then she lifted the entire affair over her head.

He forgot to breathe.

To think.

Couldn't recall his name.

She was nothing short of glorious. Long legs, full hips, a lush waist. Her breasts were large and full, tipped with hard, pink nipples that pointed upward, beckoning. Begging for his mouth. He lowered his head and kissed her there on the creamy swell of one breast, then latched on to one pebbled nipple and sucked. He may not have made love to a woman before, but he was not entirely an innocent. Lydia had taught him what pleased a woman. Unfortunately, she had also taught him a great many other lessons, none of which had proven nearly as pleasant.

But to the devil with Lydia, and to the devil with those lessons. He was breaking all his rules.

He sucked harder, eliciting a moan from Portia that went straight to his cock. She was so deliciously responsive, he could not resist teasing her other nipple as well, this time with his tongue first. He flicked over the taut bud in lazy circles, then with faster licks, and finally a gentle bite. Her fingers tunneled into his hair, and she said his name. He skimmed his hands along her waist, absorbing her heat and softness, before caressing to her thigh. He decided to go slowly, nothing more than steady strokes of his fingers up and down her hip to tantalize them both as he suckled her breast.

Her nails scored his scalp as she worked herself into a frenzy, and he loved every moment of it. The pleasure mixed with light pain as she tugged on his hair. The breathy sounds of need she made low in her throat. The way her body arched against his, seeking more. She was a wild woman, his countess, and he could not seem to get enough.

He kissed every exposed swath of flesh he could, dragging his lips over her collarbone, along her throat. Back to her mouth. She parted for him instantly, their tongues tangling as his hand slid higher, back to the decadent wetness of her cunny. She was slick and smooth and he could scarcely rein in the impulse to thrust his greedy cock inside her now.

He found her pearl and stroked over it, lightly at first, and then with greater pressure as she rocked against him, seeking more. Still kissing her hungrily, he moved nearer, the bedclothes abrading his cock to remind him that she had freed him from his trousers. And she had wanted to take him in her mouth.

*Damn.* The mere notion was enough to send a surge of raw, powerful lust straight through him. The thought of Portia's pretty pink lips wrapped around him... No, he could not contemplate it, or he would spend here and now, like the novice he was.

Instead, he turned his mind solely over to pleasing her. To listening to her sounds and following the movement of her body that showed him what she liked. When to tease, when to flutter slowly over her clitoris and when to stroke her harder. He found a particularly sensitive place and lingered there, teasing her with relentless pressure until she was gasping into his mouth and shuddering against him. New wetness coated his fingers and he worked her, drawing out her orgasm as long as he possibly could.

He had brought her off again, just as he had in the office.

The knowledge made his prick stiffer than a fire poker. He was raging to be inside her. Although Wolf had told himself he had not chosen to remain here with her for a few forbidden hours to make love to her, he knew he had been lying to himself. And now that he'd made her spend, he wanted to know what she tasted like.

He dropped to his knees on the carpets, hands on her

inner thighs as he coaxed them wider. Until she was displayed for him, pink and glistening and so damn tempting, the scent of her desire musky and tantalizing. Wolf placed a kiss on her knee, then kissed a path higher, worshiping her with his mouth. Her skin was silken and warm, and when he reached her quim, he licked along her seam, lapping up some of the evidence of her pleasure. She tasted sweet, so bloody sweet.

With a groan of surrender, he delved between her folds, licking and savoring every husky cry of passion she made, each buck of her hips. He lashed her swollen pearl with his tongue, then sucked as he had her nipple, wondering if she would be every bit as sensitive here.

And she was.

She clutched his forearms and made a keening, lusty sound as she rocked against his face. He lost himself to sensation, the taste of her on his tongue, the scent of her, heady and fragrant, the glide of her slick cunny against his lips. She was hot and wet and perfect, so perfect. He continued on, licking and sucking, fucking into her with his tongue in short strokes that made her gasp with pleasure, until she came apart again with a violent cry, the force of her passion making her body go stiff beneath his hands and lips.

He kissed her inner thigh and rocked back on his heels, meeting her gaze. Above him, she was a lusty goddess, her emerald gaze vibrant, chestnut hair wild as it tumbled around her shoulders, her breasts heaving with her every ragged breath. Her lips were parted, her eyes glazed with passion.

"I could lick your sweet cunny forever," he told her, his voice rough, a reflection of the way he felt on the inside. She had undone him, this woman, and with scarcely any effort.

"I need you inside me now," she said. "Please."

How was he to deny such a pretty plea?

He had not stopped to shed his boots or his trousers in full. This was not at all how he had intended to proceed this evening. But he was well beyond the point of concerning himself with the proper methods of seduction.

"Come here," he told her, cupping her delectable arse in his hands and guiding her to the edge of the bed. "Wrap your legs around my waist."

It seemed the most efficient means of giving them both what they wanted. There was no time to fully disrobe. No time to recline on the bed. He had to be inside her.

Now.

And Portia herself, it would seem, was guided by a similarly frantic desire. She hitched her legs around him as he had suggested, bringing her wet heat flush against his aching cockstand. He knew a fleeting moment of concern, hoping he would not disappoint her or disgrace himself. But then, his body took control. Gripping himself, he brushed the head of his cock over her quim. The kiss of her warm, slick flesh on his was enough to spur him on.

He found her cunny as if he had always been meant to, as if it were where he belonged. When he slid inside her, the grip of her was so perfect, he had to grit his teeth to stave off the urge to slam deep and hard.

"Christ, you feel good," he managed tautly, holding himself still, so still.

"You feel wonderful," she returned, clinging to his shoulders, her hair cascading down her back in wild disarray. "Why did you stop?"

Movement, aye. That was the way of it. He knew that. Had fantasized about it. *Hell*, he'd even *seen* it on numerous occasions when he'd happened upon a doxy and a drunken swill frantically shagging in the darkened alleys of the rookeries. But this was new, and while he had never before made love to a woman, he also knew that he would never again make love to another who enthralled him the way Portia did.

Two days, and he was hers. Irrevocably. Utterly. He'd never felt anything like it.

Still holding her hips, he thrust forward, until he was fully sheathed, deep inside her.

"Better?" he ground out.

"Oh yes," she whispered.

There she was, nude and beautiful, his lovely countess with his cock inside her. Wolf took a moment to savor the sight of her, all creamy and pink, the satiny flow of her hair, the elongated nipples he had sucked, the expensive counterpane and elegance of the chamber reminding him who she was and who he was and why this was so very wrong. Deliciously, beautifully wrong.

He lost control then. Fully gave himself over to the instinct roaring through him to thrust in and out. *God*, she felt like everything he had ever imagined, only a bloody thousand times more wondrous. He leaned back as he fucked her, watching as his cock moved slickly in her juices, in and out of her cunny, her breasts jiggling with each thrust. And it was so damned erotic, he was going to spend before he was ready. He never wanted this to end, wanted to go on like this forever.

"You have to...withdraw," she gasped out through ragged breaths. "Before you..."

Aye, he knew what she was after. He had brothers. They talked.

"You needn't worry, Countess," he reassured her, dropping a kiss to the bared curve of her shoulder. "I'll protect you."

*Always*, he wanted to say, but didn't. It was a foolish promise, for his place in her life was temporary. They both knew it.

He didn't want to think about that just now. So he dipped his head lower and took one of her hungry nipples into his mouth, sucking hard as he thrust into her again and again. She tightened on him almost instantly, quietly crying out and throwing her head back. Wolf allowed himself another thrust before withdrawing. Taking his cock in his hand, he spent, heart pounding, the rush so exquisite he feared he might collapse with the overwhelming power of it. He sent pearlescent spurts all over her belly before collapsing atop her on the bed.

~

Portia woke to the darkness of the night and a soft rustle of bedclothes, movement on her bed caused by another. It was at once strange and yet comforting, until her sleep-fogged mind recognized the source and the reason. *Wolf.* Her body still hummed with the pleasure he had given her, the first time and then again before they had both fallen into a sated sleep.

The second time had been slower, less frenzied. Every bit as wonderful. He had held her close and kissed her sweetly as they had both reached their completion. And once more, he had withdrawn before spending. Her ill-fated liaison with Landringham had taught her enough to know never again to be so foolish with a man. She was grateful, every day, for her son. However, as a widow of a year, if she were to fall with child, it would be obvious to everyone that Blakewell had not been the father.

Wolf pressed a kiss to her temple now, jolting her from her madly whirring thoughts. "I must go."

She swallowed down the urge to tell him to stay. Doing so would be foolish and reckless. And she had already proven both of those traits earlier when she had given in to the passion that had once ruled her. She had known, from the moment she had invited him to remain with her for a few, stolen hours, that their time together had to be finite. Far too much was at stake.

Instead of burdening him with her worries, however, she kissed his cheek. "You will take care that no one sees you?"

"Of course, Countess. I told you I'll protect you, and I mean to."

Her title felt a bit like a rebuke after the intimacies they had shared. It occurred to her what he must think. He was leaving her, and her only concern appeared to be over whether or not her servants would witness him departing from her home.

She reached for him, regret slicing through her that they could never have more than this night. "Wolf."

He paused, the glow of the fire in the grate illumining him slightly, though not nearly enough for her satisfaction. How she wished for the brace of candles to be blazing once more, that she might enjoy one more glimpse of his handsome face.

"You needn't fear. I'll sneak away same as how I found my way in."

His low reassurance was troubling, for it reminded her that it was either frightfully easy for her home to be broken into, or he was deceptively good at the criminal act. Neither of which prospect seemed a particularly heartening one. She decided to discuss the matter with Riggs in the morning in as nonchalant a fashion as she might adopt.

But that wasn't her concern at the moment. Her concern was Wolf. Because he was leaving, and she was filled with emotions she could neither convey nor properly voice.

"Thank you," she said quietly, the words falling between them in the darkness where it already seemed the closeness of hours before had begun to dissipate. "I want you to know this was a first for me as well. This is the first time I have... lain with a man since my son was conceived."

She did not want to say *made love*. Referring to the furtive couplings she had known with Landringham thusly would be wrong. Oh, she had believed herself in love with him. But he had disabused her of that notion when he had proven how dishonorable and callous he was. She had never been anything more than a diversion to him.

Silence fell, punctuated by nothing more than the ticking of the mantel clock and the steady rise and fall of their breaths. For a moment, she feared she had said too much. But then Wolf's head bent toward hers and he kissed her softly, tenderly on the lips.

"No," he said, his voice husky as he withdrew. "Thank *you*. This was a night I'll never forget."

She felt the same. Her heart was heavy as she reached for him then, taking him in her arms for one last embrace. "Nor shall I."

A sob threatened to rise up her throat, but she tamped it down, telling herself it was silly. That she could not possibly feel such a depth of affection for a man she had scarcely grown to know over the course of two days. And yet, she could not deny that there was something about him that felt so unbearably right.

He returned her embrace, pressing his cheek to the top of her head, his hand sweeping up and down her bare spine. The bedclothes had fallen to her waist, but she hadn't a care for modesty. She burrowed into the warm strength of his bare chest and wished she could remain there. Instead, she inhaled deeply of his scent, holding it in her lungs as if she could forever keep it.

"I have to go, Portia," he said quietly. "Too much longer, and someone could see."

He was right, of course. She could not spend all night

clinging to him, refusing to let him leave. She swallowed down the emotions welling, torturous emotions she had no right to feel in regards to this East End stranger.

He released her and slipped from the bed, moving in the shadows with the ease of a man who was accustomed to stalking through the night in darkness. Portia hugged herself as she watched him calmly don his garments. Subtle movements, the slide of fabric, the shifting of his long limbs. It seemed to her that he had just begun when he stilled, apparently having finished completing his dress.

"Until we meet again," he whispered.

Portia watched his shadow move through her chamber, crossing to the door, before disappearing.

She did not have the heart to tell him there would be no meeting again.

## CHAPTER 8

"You've finally decided to join us, your lordship?"

Wolf grimaced at his eldest brother Jasper's taunting query as he met his brothers for a morning meeting in the office at The Sinner's Palace. The same office where, mere days before, he had first seen Portia. Had kissed her. And there, upon the big desk with its carved lion legs, he had raised her hems and—

"Come now, no need to provoke hisnabs," his brother Rafe added, further intruding upon Wolf's thoughts.

Which was for the best, he knew. He needed to concern himself with the business at hand rather than the woman who had unexpectedly overtaken his life like a raging summer storm.

"We humbly thank you for honoring us with your presence, Your Grace," Hart inserted with a chortle.

Wolf pinned all three of his brothers with a chastising glare. "That'll be enough from you. I'll thank you to remember I'm not the one who's gone off and found himself caught in the parson's mousetrap with a rum mort."

"I haven't been caught just yet," Hart reminded him, his

expression rueful. "I'm still bleeding *courting*."

Hart's efforts to keep his betrothed, Lady Emma Morgan, free from scandal were honorable, even if they did appear to nettle.

"Good as married," Wolf said with a shrug, because that was also true.

Everyone knew Hart had been unable to resist Lady Emma from the moment he had seen her.

*Christ, that rather sounds familiar.* Wolf frowned and rubbed a hand over his jaw, not liking this new direction of his thoughts one whit more than the last.

"And yet the three of us have managed to arrive in a timely fashion despite our marriages—impending and otherwise—to great ladies," Jasper drawled.

It was true that his brothers had all married, or were about to marry, in Hart's case, into the quality. First Jasper, who had managed to ensnare his wife Lady Octavia in rather unconventional means. Then Rafe, who had thought he had fallen in love with a governess only to discover she was a lady hiding her true identity for fear of her arsehole guardian. And finally Hart, who through equally unconventional methods had orchestrated a plot to uncover more information about their missing brother Logan and had ended up with Lady Emma Morgan as his betrothed along the way.

But his pointed rejoinders aside, Wolf couldn't ignore the three pairs of eyes trained on him. His brothers were awaiting an answer, curse them. It was not like him to sleep late. Despite his penchant for staying up through the night, when there was a meeting concerning the operations of their gaming hell, Wolf had never been tardy. Not once.

"I'm a growing lad," he suggested, for he was the tallest and broadest of them all.

His brutish size had always suited him. And it would

stand him in good stead when he found out who was responsible for that bruise on Portia's cheek.

"Aye, growing." Rafe grinned and patted his own lean belly. "Too many honey cakes?"

Wolf scowled. "Why the devil are you all against me today? And where are our sisters?"

Their sisters, Caro, Pen, and Lily were ordinarily in attendance at their weekly meetings.

"Caro sent word that she needs to rest today," Jasper answered. "'Tis soon time for the babe to arrive, and after she had to dash here to tend to Hart's sorry arse, she deserves a respite. Pen is busy with a few matters at The Sinner's Palace II, and Lily is…damn, where is Lily?"

He addressed the question to the room at large.

"Damned if I know," Rafe said.

"I've no bleeding idea," Hart offered.

His brothers' eyes swung to Wolf.

"Don't tell me you've lost her," he growled. "I'm gone for one bloody night, and the whole place is done up when I return."

Hart raised a brow. "*You* were gone for a night?"

"Have you finally tupped the proprietress of The Beggar's Purse, then?" Rafe asked mildly. "We were all beginning to wonder when you'd grow a pair of tallywags and bed a wench."

"Oh, he's definitely bedded a wench," Jasper said slyly before Wolf could deny the claim. "Felicitations, lad. You're finally a man."

His ears went hot. "Blast you all. I didn't tup the proprietress of The Beggar's Purse. She's a friend and nothing more."

"A friend who looks at you as if she wants to—"

"Enough," he bit out, silencing Hart, who never knew when to still his damned tongue. "I didn't bed her."

The proprietress of the rather ramshackle establishment known as The Beggar's Purse was a familiar of Wolf's. But although she had hinted at her interest in making their friendship something more, he had always hesitated to accept her offer of companionship. Lydia's defection had left him convinced he did not need a woman in his life or in his bed. And he had governed his life in accordance with that knowledge.

Until Portia.

"But you *did* bed someone." Jasper's tone, like his gaze, was shrewd.

The eldest of the Sutton clan always seemed to know more than he should.

Wolf's face flamed. *Christ*, he could feel it. He was *blushing*.

"Stubble it," he growled. "I'll not be speaking another word of my private affairs with you. With any of you. Haven't we a business to run and a rogue brother to fret over? Surely those two worries are of far greater import."

"Wolf's right," Rafe allowed, unable to suppress a rascal's grin. "It ain't any of our concern if he's playing blanket hornpipe or who he chooses to play it with. Although, brother, may I offer my felicitations on the loss of your—"

Wolf punched Rafe in the shoulder, effectively ending his teasing. "I told you to hold your bloody tongue. If you'd like me to start making crude jokes about you and Lady Persephone, I'd be more than happy to."

He sounded formal and stiff and indignant, even to his own ears. But curse his brothers, Wolf had no wish to be the subject of this discussion for a moment longer. Because Portia was... She was his, damn it. And he had vowed to protect her. And making love to her had most definitely not been a trifling matter.

"Ah," Rafe said simply, the lone word laden with much

meaning.

Meaning Wolf also did not like, because it seemed to suggest more than he was willing to admit where Portia was concerned.

"Aye," he groused, frowning at all his brothers. "I slept late. That is all."

"Of course." Jasper nodded, looking as if he were attempting to fight a smile of his own before issuing a heavy sigh. "Business matters first, then. The Sinner's Palace II will be ready to open in a sennight, as planned. Pen has done an admirable job at making certain the establishment is as princely as possible, and we're down to only needing to hire a few more hands. I trust matters here have been proceeding smoothly since my last visit?"

Between Jasper's marriage to Lady Octavia, being a father to his twin daughters, and managing the opening of the second Sinner's Palace in the West End, Jasper's visits to the East End establishment that had begun their family empire had grown fewer and sparser in recent months. Hart and Wolf had been happy to take up where their brother had left off, however. Wolf enjoyed running the daily operations.

"As smooth as a babe's arse," Wolf muttered, still vexed with his siblings.

"Excellent." Jasper's expression turned grim. "Then let us proceed to the most important matter of all."

"Loge," Hart said needlessly.

Their brother was never far from any of their minds. Not when they had believed him dead, and most certainly not now that they knew him to be alive.

"I've heard back from the men I've engaged to make discreet inquiries about Archer Tierney and Mr. Martin," Jasper said. "It would seem moneylending ain't all that's being practiced at Tierney's establishment."

That was what Wolf had feared. A sinister feeling swept

through him. "What do you mean, it ain't all?"

"I'm not certain yet," Jasper answered slowly, passing a hand over his jaw in a weary gesture Wolf recognized, for he often made it himself; it was a Sutton trait. "What I do know is that if Loge was willing to abandon this family as he did, there's got to be sufficient reason. It means he is involved in something that's dangerous for either him or for us, or for all of us."

Something dangerous. It made sense. But what?

"What the bleeding hell could be more dangerous than running a gaming hell in the East End and contending with bloodthirsty bastards like the Bradleys?" Hart asked, giving voice to the questions in Wolf's own mind.

Hart had recently been stabbed in a fray with the Bradleys, the family who owned a rival gaming hell. Despite Wolf's best efforts at sewing him up, Hart's wound had become infected, and if not for the intervention of their sister Caro, they would have lost him. No one knew better than Hart just how dangerous the damned Bradleys were.

"That's what troubles me," Jasper admitted, worry evident in his voice and his countenance both. "I aim to go to Tierney's place myself, to see if there's anything I can find out."

"I'll accompany you," Wolf volunteered.

"And me," said Rafe.

"I'm bleeding coming too," Hart offered almost in unison. "If danger is involved, then you aren't going alone. I'll be damned if I lose another brother."

"Here now." Jasper raised a dark brow. "Did I say I'd be needing accompaniment? Do I look like a granny who needs to be protected?"

Wolf cocked his head. "You *are* getting a bit gray at the temples. And quite domesticated now that Lady Octavia is leading you about by the nutmegs."

"Quite full of yourself now that you've tupped your first

wench, ain't you?" Jasper returned.

Blast his brothers. They were a curse and a blessing all at once.

"I didn't tup anyone," he snapped.

Because *tupping* was a paltry way of describing what had happened last night. And Portia was not just any wench, whose name was to be bandied about. She was…special. But he'd sooner strut bare-arsed through the gaming rooms than admit that to the trio of beloved scoundrels facing him now.

"Of course you didn't," Rafe said, his tone making it clear that Wolf wasn't believed.

That was bloody fine. They could suspect all they wished, but that didn't mean he was going to tell them a damned thing. Portia was his.

Not his.

Not truly.

She was a widowed countess with a young son who was the earl, and she had someone in her life giving her cause to fear. The reminder set his teeth on edge and had him grinding his molars. But there was nothing he could do to aid her here and now.

"When do you propose we go to Tierney's?" he asked Jasper instead of addressing his brothers' thinly veiled innuendos.

"Tomorrow seems as good a day as any," Jasper said. "I've men watching Tierney's and Loge's every move, and they'll let me know if anything changes."

Hart nodded. "Excellent plan. We can't afford to let Tierney slip away, and now that we've found Loge, we can't lose him."

And hopefully, they could convince him to return to the family, regardless of what he had done and what dangers he faced. They were Suttons first, and they were loyal to each other. That had to count for something.

At least, Wolf hoped it did.

"It's settled then," Rafe agreed. "Tomorrow, we infiltrate that den of thieves and bring our brother out kicking and screaming if we must."

"We'll manage," Jasper said tightly. "Now then, I suppose we ought to find our youngest sister."

"What manner of trouble could she be in?" Rafe asked. "Our Lily is an angel."

Wolf was reasonably sure there was nothing angelic about what Lily had been doing in secret, particularly at Bellingham and Co., but he refrained from voicing his concerns. After all, whatever Loge was involved in was likely far, far worse than any manner of mischief Lily could entangle herself in. And Wolf had a countess to worry over now.

He had to find a way to help protect Portia.

And to see her again.

Soon.

~

"Mama?"

Portia blinked, startled from her thoughts by Edwin, who had arrived in her sitting room as was customary each morning following breakfast, before the day's studies commenced.

"Darling," she greeted him, rising from her chair and extending her arms for an embrace.

As always, he bounded into her arms with a boyish enthusiasm she knew in her mother's heart that life would one day take away from him. And so, she held him close, burying her face in the carefully combed hair the same shade of chestnut as hers, relishing his love and the sweet scent of him.

It seemed to her that her son squeezed her waist with extra enthusiasm this morning, and she knew a sharp spear of guilt at her selfishness the night before. She had risked so very much when she had asked Wolf to stay. Because despite his continued insistence he would protect her, nothing and no one could save her from her brother's wrath. She shuddered to think what actions he would take if she were to incur his fury any further than she had already done in her inglorious past and her trip to The Sinner's Palace. He had threatened her with taking Edwin, and she knew he would do just that and anything else to bring her misery.

She kissed Edwin's crown as she so oft did, tamping down the worry that was never far from her heart. "And how is my favorite son this fine morning?"

He giggled. "Mama, I am your only son. It is a matter of course that I must also be your favorite. I haven't any competition."

She smiled, his hair, already wayward from their embrace tickling her cheek. It seemed her son had only to blink his eyes and his tidy hair began to wave and curl as it was naturally wont to do. "My favorite person, then. How is that? You are my very favorite person in all the world, you know."

He gave her another squeeze before releasing her and taking a step back. "That is a heavy mantle indeed to wear about one's shoulders."

Her heart gave a little pang as he stood before her. He was growing so tall. It seemed only yesterday he had been a babe she had swaddled and held in her arms. Sometimes, she wished she could pause time, even just for a while, so that she could prolong the joy of his childhood. Her life had possessed precious little happiness, and what she had known thus far had been all Edwin.

And now, Wolf.

The thought gave her pause, for it felt...not just foreign,

but disloyal. How could a man she scarcely knew have caused her happiness? It seemed impossible. And yet, she could not deny the glow she had felt this morning when she had risen, thinking of him. A glow which had promptly been doused when her rational mind recalled last night's recklessness must never be repeated.

She cleared her throat against a sudden, stinging rush of tears, both at her son's growing up before her eyes and what she could never have. "Nonetheless, it is a mantle you wear well."

Her son ducked his head, then cast her a sheepish glance from beneath lowered lashes, a pose that was quite familiar by now. "Are you vexed with me, Mama?"

"Vexed is perhaps a strong word," she said sternly, knowing she could not allow him to run roughshod over the household and do as he pleased, yet hating to be firm as she must. "Disappointed, however, yes. It was not well done of you to go sneaking about the library when you were meant to be asleep."

"I am sorry, Mama." Edwin hung his head once more.

"I trust you shan't be doing it again," she said pointedly, for though she had scolded him the night before, she had also done so before Wolf.

And she had been thoroughly flustered by his unexpected appearance.

*Good heavens*, that reminded her. She truly did need to speak to Riggs about the possibility of a housebreak occurring. They had to be certain all the doors and windows were soundly fastened each evening.

Still, something told her Wolf Sutton was no ordinary housebreaker, and that his finding entry did not necessarily suggest others would as well.

"I'll not be doing it again, Mama. I promised last night that I would not."

Yes, he had. But she knew her son well enough to suspect he may be tempted to break his promise.

"If you wish to spend more time on your drawings, perhaps I can arrange for Mr. Leslie to conclude your lessons one quarter hour early each day so that you may do so," she allowed, for she would prefer to be able to watch over her son rather than fear he would wander about in the dark.

The mere thought of him attempting to slide down a banister on his way to the library set her protective motherly instincts on edge. He could break his leg, or worse, his neck. Only heaven knew what mischief young lads made when they were sneaking about in the night, unattended.

But rather than being pleased by her suggestion—a compromise to keep him from further trouble—Edwin frowned. "But Uncle says I am behind in my studies and I am to add an additional hour to them every day. Mr. Leslie said so."

The knowledge that her brother was intruding in her son's studies sent outrage knifing through Portia. It was bad enough he had insisted upon selecting the tutor himself, a man she felt was far too rigid and cold to be a tutor who would encourage Edwin's learning. But now he was intervening to suggest they lengthen his studies?

Perhaps Mr. Leslie needed to be reminded who it was that employed him.

But just as quickly as that indignant thought occurred to her, all the fight in her deflated as she recalled her situation. Granville's hands were in everything. She had no true power or will of her own. Her entire life, and that of her son, was ruled over by a tyrant who despised her for the indiscretions of her youth.

"When did you speak with your uncle?" she asked instead of giving voice to the myriad of emotion swirling through her.

Portia took great care to keep her brother's true nature from Edwin. As long as his rage was directed at her rather than her son, she saw no need to worry the boy.

"Yesterday when he paid a call," Edwin answered. "He said he had come to visit you as well."

Yes, much to her regret, he had. She wondered if Granville had visited Edwin before or after he had smashed her inkwell and slapped her. She supposed it did not matter, but she disliked the notion of him going to her son when still in one of his rages. She did not think him capable of raising a hand to a child, but then, she had once not believed him capable of many sins she now knew he was.

And whilst she could not protect herself from her brother's violence, she would do everything in her power to protect her son.

"Lord Granville did indeed visit me yesterday," she said, endeavoring to keep her tone mild and to reveal none of the loathing she felt for her brother to Edwin.

The stain he had left behind was yet upon her lovely wall, and the bruise he had left on her cheek had been an ugly reminder she'd needed to conceal with Pear's Almond Bloom again. The paper-hangings would need to be replaced.

She tore her gaze away, but it was too late. Edwin's curious stare was fixed upon the terribly besmirched paper-hangings, which the housekeeper had done her utmost to repair following the incident Portia had halfheartedly explained.

"What happened to the paper-hangings?" her son asked.

"Nothing you need to fret over, darling," she said brightly. "I do believe it is time for your studies to begin with Mr. Leslie. You ought to run along so you are not tardy."

"It looks as if the ink from your inkwell spilled down the wall," he observed.

Because it had. Because some terrible tyrant had hurled it

there so that it would shatter.

She patted her son on the back in a gesture meant to comfort. "It was an accident. One of the maids unintentionally overset it."

That was a lie, and one that made precious little sense, but she could only hope he would not ask further questions.

Edwin frowned at the wall.

"Go on," she urged him. "Mr. Leslie will be wondering where you are."

"Yes, Mama," he said at last, performing a reasonably elegant bow for a lad of his tender years.

She watched him hasten from the room, taking part of her heart with her, and then allowed herself to drift into her thoughts yet again. Thoughts that were quite unlike the ones which usually occupied her mind. Thoughts of Wolf.

Of his clever lips on hers.

His skillful hands on her body.

Of him, deep inside her, their bodies joined.

She had been the first woman to whom he had made love, and she could not seem to crush the fierce, possessive pride that knowledge sent through her by the cheerful light of the morning. She needed to do something else, to seek diversion by some other means.

A discreet knock at the door distracted her as if on cue. She turned from her listless pacing of the carpets.

"Come," she called.

It was Riggs, the butler bearing his customary morning salver containing her correspondence. "Your letters, my lady."

"Thank you. In the ordinary place, if you please." She moved to the window, gazing unseeing down at the street below while Riggs laid out the morning arrivals. "Riggs, are you certain all the windows and doors are secure here at Blakewell House?"

"Of course, my lady," he intoned.

She wondered for a brief moment if the butler were the source of Granville's information. But no, she did not like to think it, for he had been quite loyal and good to her through all the years of her marriage.

"Thank you," she said, turning to him with as much of a smile as she could muster. "That will be all."

The butler's gaze slipped over her shoulder, and she knew he was looking at the stained paper-hanging. But to his credit, he said not a word about it. With a bow, he withdrew from the chamber, leaving her alone yet again.

Thinking that her correspondence ought to at least prove some small manner of distraction, she moved to her writing desk where it awaited her and seated herself. Calmly, Portia began the morning ritual that had always been a source of great satisfaction. A letter from Blakewell's sister, Lady Jane, an invitation to a musicale from the Countess of Rayne, and a letter from her old friend, the Duchess of Montrose, reminding her about her ball three days hence.

Then a missive in shaky scratch she recognized, for it belonged to Mrs. Courteney, Avery's mother. *Avery needs your help*, it read. *I beg you, do not forsake him.* Her heart gave a pang at the notion her half brother was in some manner of trouble, until her eye chanced to the next paragraph, where Mrs. Courteney requested the sum of one hundred pounds, on behalf of her son, that she might aid him in his *difficulties*.

Suspicion cut through her, the same suspicion that had led her to The Sinner's Palace, chasing after her long-lost brother. If Avery was indeed alive and well, and if he were truly in need of assistance, Portia would be more than happy to help him however she could, as long as she was able to keep her efforts from Granville. However, she was beginning to suspect Avery's mother was lying for her own prospective gain.

Frowning, Portia set aside the note from Mrs. Courteney and reached for the last missive on the bottom of the tidy pile. And it was that letter, far more than the others, which made her heart pound with secret pleasure and her face suffuse with heat.

In a pronounced masculine scrawl, it simply read *My offer still stands.*

Although it was unsigned, no doubt in an effort to save her from prying eyes or speculation, Portia knew who had written the letter. *Wolf.* With a trembling hand, she raised the letter to her nose, hoping to inhale a hint of him, however small and brief. Unfortunately, there was not a trace of citrus and musk.

His offer.

What was he implying?

*Had* he made her an offer? Most certainly not to be his mistress, which was out of the question, and nor to be his wife, which was equally impossible, and would have been utterly foolish given they had only known each other for the span of two days. What, then?

She missed him. He had only been gone for hours, and yet the sight of his bold penmanship and the knowledge he had thought about her enough to pen her a note and send it to her so that it would arrive this morning increased her longing for him.

"Oh, Wolf," she whispered, staring down at the letters until they swirled before her eyes.

What if she could see Wolf one more time? It would not be purely selfish if she sought his help, would it?

No answers came to her save one.

An equally impossible one, it was true. Daring, reckless, and utterly foolish. She could not do it. There was no way.

Or could she?

## CHAPTER 9

Wolf wondered if the blasted missive had caused her problems.

Sending it had been selfish and careless, and Wolf had recognized it the moment the lad he had paid to deliver it to Blakewell House had gone. He had intentionally been vague and had left it unsigned, which he had convinced himself ought to be sufficient to guard her from prying eyes. But by God, if he led whomever had done her violence to strike her again, he would never forgive himself. The mere thought was enough to make his gut clench and his protective instincts rebel with the need to seek immediate, swift, and bloody vengeance.

His idiocy aside, Wolf had still been hoping to hear back from her. To receive *some* acknowledgment, however small, that his missive had found its way beneath her eye. That what had transpired between them that night had meant something to her, for it had bloody well meant *everything* to him. Aye, he wanted some inkling that although days had passed since they had parted ways, she had thought of him, at least once.

Instead, he had received nothing, save silence.

Not a missive.

Not a call.

Not a hint of the woman who had taken to haunting his every sleeping and waking hour, curse her.

"Stupid arsehole," he muttered to himself below his breath as he passed Viscount Torrington and a handful of the lord's familiar cronies at a hazard table.

The viscount had nearly perished in a vicious phaeton accident that had left him, if rumor was to be believed, with an impaired memory. Although aloof and icy, he had been a regular presence at The Sinner's Palace in recent months. A nob with deep pockets and devoted resilience at the green baize was always heartily appreciated by the Suttons. Lately, the viscount had been looking rather gaunt. Wolf could only wonder at the reason.

A woman, perhaps?

Christ knew Portia was the cause of his own recent sleepless nights.

Well, her and Loge. The trip to Tierney's lair with his brothers had proven every bit as fruitless as the missive he had sent to Portia. They had arrived at the moneylender's establishment to find it empty. Not a soul within.

Loge was, once again, gone.

The men Jasper had been paying to watch Tierney and Loge had sworn on their mothers' graves that Archer Tierney and Mr. Martin, as Loge was calling himself, had entered the establishment through the rear earlier that morning. No one had left. When Wolf and his brothers had forced their way inside, they had found nary a hint of anyone.

They had torn the bloody place apart, from the bowels to the rafters, and come up with nothing and no one. Not a single damned clue as to where they had gone or how they had managed to flee without any of Jasper's men taking note. It had not been what any of them had anticipated, and the realization their brother was once again lost to them had been a staggering blow.

Not so different from Portia's silence.

"Mr. Sutton."

Wolf was jolted from his musings suddenly by the silent appearance of Hugh, one of The Sinner's Palace guards, at his side. He stopped in his slow perambulation of the room, for it was damned unlike the guard to intrude when he was on the floor.

"Is something amiss, Hugh?" he asked quietly, taking care to make certain his voice did not carry.

The Sinner's Palace rule was to keep their patrons ensconced in a world where nothing but leisure and pleasure existed. The window coverings were always closed so no one knew whether it was day or night, and there could be an entire infantry brigade formed at the front door, about to stage an assault, but everyone within would do their utmost to make certain their lofty patrons remained blissfully ignorant.

"You've a visitor," Hugh said. "Petticoats."

*Petticoats.*

A woman.

Portia? Wolf's heart leapt at the possibility.

He was instantly on edge. "Where?"

"Awaiting you in the office, sir," Hugh responded, his countenance carefully blank.

Good. Unlike his brothers, the guard knew better than to needle him about wenches.

He nodded. "Thank you, Hugh. You'll oversee the floor for me?"

"Aye, Mr. Sutton."

Hugh did not need to speak twice. Wolf fled the floor

with such haste, he nearly tripped over his feet. He would have laughed at his own eagerness had he not waited days to hear from her, but as it was, it seemed as if a lifetime had passed since he had left her in the darkest depths of the night with the hope he would see her again soon. And if it was indeed Portia who had managed to steal away at this hour of the night and find her way to him, he was half-afraid she would bolt before he would even reach her.

His heart was thundering in his chest by the time he approached the office he had taken to sharing with his brothers. The door was closed, but he did not bother to knock or otherwise announce his presence. Instead, he threw it open and bounded over the threshold like the brash East End booby he was.

A woman was indeed within, her back to him upon his entrance, and though she was gently illuminated by the wall sconces, he knew the shape of her. His hands itched with remembrance of the way those bountiful curves had felt beneath them. She whirled about as he kicked the door closed at his back.

"Portia," he said, striding toward her.

"Wolf," she cried, removing a hat and veil from her head and tossing it to the carpets as she met him halfway.

She launched herself into his chest with such unprecedented enthusiasm that he staggered back a handful of steps as he caught her against him, holding her tight. She was warm and lovely, all flashing emerald eyes and sweet pink lips smiling in welcome, and she smelled like bloody paradise, like a garden bursting to life with decadent blooms.

"Where have you been, Countess?" he asked, careful to keep his tone soft.

He would not make demands of her. Her presence in his life was a privilege, and no one knew it better than Wolf. That she was even here, in his gaming hell, in his arms, was more than enough to please him. Seeing her, being with her, made him...*happy*.

Well, bleeding hell, there it was. This woman made him feel things he'd never felt before. Things he'd never thought to feel.

"I had to wait until I could safely see you," she said, cupping his face as if he were a welcomed sight she could not quite believe she beheld. "I am meant to be at a ball this evening, but it was hosted by a friend of mine, and I was able to use one of her carriages to slip away."

*Christ*, he hated that Portia had to sneak about just to see him. With any other lady of the quality, he would have suspected it was merely the shame and possibility of scandal at it becoming known she was spending time alone with a rookeries-born ruffian like him. But he knew her fear ran far deeper than social repercussions. She feared for herself.

The knowledge ate at him, as did his inability to aid her or protect her. Even as he knew that if she refused to give him a name or a reason why, there was naught he could do. He had hesitated to make inquiries about her relatives as had been his initial instinct for fear of any further problems it would make for her. And her ensuing silence had only supported that notion.

"How long do we have?" he queried instead of addressing any of the difficulties which never loomed far from their interactions.

"An hour," she said, nibbling on her bottom lip. "Perhaps a few minutes more."

"Not enough." He lowered his forehead to hers. "Not nearly enough."

But he would take it, greedy cove that he was. Aye, he would seize it with both hands and make the most of whatever time alone with her he could manage.

"Are you upset that I've come?" Her eyes searched his, a

frown gathering her brows. "Have I interrupted your evening? I know you are a busy man, and I would have sent word had I dared, but I am risking enough by coming to you. I didn't wish to chance anyone discovering my true intentions and sending word to my—well. It matters not. Pray tell me I have not arrived at an inopportune time."

She was rambling. And damn him, but the urge to kiss her senseless was stronger than his need for a next breath. He had to tamp down his longing. Remind himself he was a man who possessed at least a shred of honor where she was concerned.

Belatedly, it occurred to him that she had nearly revealed something to him.

"Sending word to whom?" he prompted, repeating the words she had spoken before abruptly changing course.

Her gaze slid over his shoulder. "I misspoke. Have I come at the wrong time? I have no wish to importune you with my presence."

When she attempted to extricate herself from his embrace, Wolf held strong. "Cease. There is no time you could come to me that would ever be wrong, love. And nor could you importune me."

Wolf had to tamp down the disappointment rising within, that she did not trust him with her woes. That she still refused to reveal to him who it was that she feared, who had hurt her, and why. Perhaps it would come in time. He could earn her trust. Wolf well understood that it was a treasured luxury that needed to be earned rather than simply expected.

Her stare flitted back to his, the frown yet furrowing her brows. "Are you certain?"

He decided to answer her in the best way he knew, which was to dip his head and claim her mouth in a kiss. Her lips beneath his were keen and warm and soft and he could not deny himself the pleasure of sucking on the fullness of the succulent lower before devoting his attention to the Cupid's bow of her upper. From there, he could not control himself. His tongue sought entry, and she opened, tipping her head back on a breathy moan.

Ah, bloody, bloody hell, this was heaven and damnation all at once, the woman he wanted more than anything in his arms, the taste of her on his tongue, her breaths mingling with his, her arms wrapped around him, and yet he could only have her for the span of *one goddamned hour*.

He deepened the kiss, trying to show her what he could not say, the wealth of feeling that had been steeping inside him during these last few days. But despite the appalling lack of time they had ahead of them, he kissed her slowly. Lingeringly. Savoring the softness of her lips, the sweet sounds of desire she made, the way she stepped into his body, her breasts crushing into his chest. It occurred to him, as they stood entwined, hip to hip, that this woman had been made for him.

And she had come to him tonight.

Gratitude mingled with desire. She had not forgotten him as part of Wolf had feared. Like him, she must have been bitten by this same mad need, this undeniable sense of connection, as if the two of them were bonded in a way that went far beyond the simple, animalistic coupling of man and woman. Yes, his body had been joined with hers, but there was something so much bigger, so much stronger, than lust uniting them. He felt it in her kiss, in her body's reaction to him, the way she clung to him as if she were a vine, intent upon twisting herself around him and forever remaining.

If only.

No, he could not keep her here, much as he would like. He had her for the next hour. Not enough. Never enough.

Still kissing her, he moved them to the desk, guiding her slowly backward. It did not matter that at any moment, someone could unwittingly intrude upon them. All that mattered was that she was here, in his arms, and her lips were responding to his so deliciously, her hands roaming his body as if she were overwhelmed with the urge to touch him everywhere. Her fingers traveled beneath his coat, over his shoulders and down his chest. He found her waist and settled her on the desk, not giving a damn about the ledgers which were lying open, awaiting Jasper's perusal.

He dragged his mouth from hers at last, but he could not resist the tempting smoothness of her jaw, the silken heat of her cheek. Then lower. She tilted her head back, giving him easy access to her throat. His hands fisted in her skirts, lifting them, eager fingers skimming her stocking-encased calves and knees. He lifted and bunched fine fabric and petticoats, not stopping until her hems were pulled around her waist.

Wolf took a moment to remove his lips from where they feasted on her throat, just above her pounding pulse, to admire the sight of her, shapely, long legs on display.

"You are perfection," he managed.

Her kiss-bruised lips canted in a wistful smile. "All too imperfect, I fear. Otherwise, I would not be here."

"I am damned glad you are." His voice was breathless and ragged, the ferocity of the effect she had upon him too great to hide.

"I could not stay away," she confided softly.

The admission made a sharp stab of lust spear through him, almost sending him to his knees. Which would not have been a terrible place, given that it would have positioned his mouth conveniently near to her cunny.

"You need to attend more balls," he growled, and then he could not resist sliding her legs apart and insinuating himself between them.

He was rigid and ready for her, and when he stepped forward, it brought his cockstand flush with the decadent heat of her quim. Just barely, he suppressed the urge to thrust against her like a mad, rutting beast. Now that he'd had her once, he could not get his fill. But he had no notion of why she had come to him tonight. Had it been for this?

"I need you." Her throaty voice was all the reassurance he required. "Please, Wolf."

Her fingers were on the fall of his trousers between them now, and when she grazed the head of his prick, he nearly spent then and there, even with a layer of fabric between them.

He ground himself against her palm. "Tell me what you want."

He was prolonging the torture, he knew, but there was something about her elegant aristocratic lips saying every bawdy thing she wanted him to do to her that made him harder than an anvil.

Her eyes were dark with emerald fire, and he thought he could happily drown in them. Aye, he was that far gone, thinking maudlin, bloody mad thoughts for her, heart galloping in his chest, breath ragged. His lungs threatened to burst from his body.

"I want you inside me," she said.

He groaned, hips blindly chasing those wicked fingers as he took her lips with his once more. She opened, her tongue dancing with his, and this time, he recognized the tart, sugary sweetness of her as lemonade. He sucked on her tongue and then withdrew to kiss the corner of her lips, dragging his mouth along her jaw until he found her ear.

"More," he whispered, tonguing the delicate whorl, nibbling on the arch until she shivered. "Tell me more, Countess."

She traced the ridge of his cock boldly, then hooked her leg around his hips, drawing him more firmly against her. "I ache for you, Wolf. You've all I've been able to think about."

"Only me?" he nipped her neck lightly, then raised his head, taking in how lovely she looked, her hair carefully arranged, a parure of pink gemstones glistening from her throat and ears and even from somewhere in the depths of her luxurious chestnut curls. The gems were in a setting of gold, fashioned to look as if they were flowers.

He'd give his last halfpenny to see her nude, wearing nothing but her jewels.

"Only you," she confirmed.

He skimmed his hand above her garters, along the bare, velvety flesh of her inner thigh. "Are you ready?"

"Touch me."

Her invitation was bold, issued as she watched him with her Siren's allure from beneath lowered lashes. Holding her gaze, he trailed his touch higher, until her wet heat kissed his seeking fingertips. And then, because he couldn't not, he stepped back to admire her, breasts thrust high above her bodice, looking all flushed and pretty, his fingers stroking over her as her lips fell open.

"Christ," he hissed, for she was wet and hot and so damned tempting. "You are, aren't you, love?"

She undid the fall of his trousers in response and his cock sprang free, demanding and unapologetically crude. Portia did not appear to mind, for she took him in hand, her fingers closing in a tight hold that had more breath seeping from his lungs, until he was dizzied. Overcome by the heady mix of lust and longing. A drop of mettle had already seeped from the tip of him, so desperate was his want, and she slicked it over him with her thumb, making him groan.

But instead of driving into her as his every heightened instinct commanded, he parted her folds, finding the plump heat of her pearl. Recalling what had garnered the most response from her, he applied pressure, swirling over the little bud until she was panting, her breaths leaving her in ragged gasps. Watching her come apart for him made the wait worthwhile.

He moved faster, gaining confidence, watching her gasp and writhe as he pleasured her, feeling her hips pumping, chasing his touch. And just when he sensed she was about to reach her pinnacle, he traced her hot folds lower, finding her entrance. He slid his forefinger into her cunny. The grip of her inner walls was tantalizing. He knew how incendiary that tight sheath felt on his cock, and he could not wait to feel it again. But he wanted to make her spend first, before he entered her. Wanted her desperate.

"Wolf," she moaned his name as she surrendered to the pleasure he gave her.

Unrelenting, he worked her clitoris with his thumb while he pumped a finger inside her. But it was not enough, because he was being denied those plump, wonderful breasts of hers, tucked away inside her bodice. He trapped her hems in place with his hip, pinning them to the desk, and with his hand now free to roam, he reached for her bodice, tugging it down until her breasts spilled over the top, full and ripe.

As he worked his finger in and out of her, he bent, taking her nipple in his mouth and sucking. She came on a keening cry, her cunny tightening around his finger in delicious spasms as he continued fucking her. Ravenous, he moved to her other breast, licking and sucking and nipping until the last ripple of pleasure had been drawn from her.

Only then did he shift nearer, so the head of his cock brushed over her wet folds. She gasped, her eyes, which had drifted closed during the height of her orgasm, fluttering open, her green gaze burning into his.

"Put me inside you," he told her, for her fingers were still wrapped firmly around his cock, and he wanted her to take control of him and her pleasure both.

She guided him to her pulsing cunny. Grasping him

firmly, she dipped his cock inside. Molten heat engulfed him, and it was agony, sweet, searing agony, to hold still and allow her to have her way with him. But it was also excruciatingly delicious. Here she was, his brave and bold countess, seizing what she wanted.

And what she wanted was him.

Pride swelled, challenging the effervescent lust boiling to almost painful fury within. She felt so good around him. But he remained where he was, chest falling in uneven breaths, waiting until she drew him forward.

"Deeper," she said breathlessly. "I need you all the way inside me, Wolf."

At her request, what could he do but obey? Wolf's hips were moving before his mind could sufficiently process her words. One thrust, and he was lodged deep, and she was completely surrounding him with her heat, constricting on him. It was—dare he think it—better than the first time. Because she was commanding him, and he was hers to do with as she wished.

"You feel so damned good," he ground out, relishing the sensation of her wrapped around him, bathing his cock in her wetness.

"Yes," she said softly, clutching tightly at his shoulders as she urged him on.

From there, his body once more told him what to do. He began moving, tentatively at first, sliding almost completely from her only to sink deep again. The pleasure was exquisite, and he was as tightly wound as the coil of a pocket watch spring. But he wanted to prolong their coupling. To make it last for as long as possible.

Except, this was all still new to him. Not just making love to a woman, but the way that woman made him feel. And not merely the way she made his cock feel, either. There was far more to what they shared than physicality. It was the way she made his... *Christ*, the way she made his heart feel, too.

But he did not want to think about that now.

No, he wanted to devote himself to giving her pleasure. To making her come. He'd heard coves brag about their prowess. How quickly they could have a woman shattering in their arms. But he had never known how powerful he would feel, knowing he had given her the same bliss that coursed through him when he was inside her.

He moved faster, their bodies joined and yet sliding sinuously together. And then he moved into her harder, realizing it felt good to the both of them, taking cues from her breathy sighs and the way she moved with him. He lost himself, sinking into her again and again.

She was clinging to him, cheeks flushed, her coiffure coming undone, those gems glinting in the candlelight from her throat and ears. She looked like a bloody queen, and she felt like one too, her cunny clenching on his cock, all velvet and silk. And he was going to lose control and spend inside her if he didn't take care.

But first, he needed to pay attention to her hungry nipples. They were thrust toward him in an erotic offering he could not deny. Wolf dipped his head and took a stiff peak into his mouth. She cried out as he took a long, hearty suckle, her nails digging into his shoulders and raking down his chest in a score he felt through the layers of his clothes. It occurred to him what a travesty it was, not having her fully naked and not being nude himself, but almost entirely clothed. Oh to have the leisure to enjoy her as she deserved, worshiping every bit of creamy skin he could set his hands, lips, and tongue upon.

He would settle for this, for whatever he could get from her, even if stolen moments, the both of them still dressed, was all she was willing to offer. She had come to him, and she was here, and he was inside her, damn it, and nothing had ever felt so perfect and right, and neither had he.

Her orgasm took him by surprise. Her cunny clenched on him with a sudden strength that he had not expected. Tremors of pleasure shuddered through her, making her tighten and throb around his cock. He moved to her other breast, sucking the hard bud, catching it between his teeth and tugging. All sense of control fled. His restraint was gone.

His own rush of pleasure, when it hit him, was also without warning. The pressure in his ballocks burst, and then he had a moment to think, to remind himself he could not afford to get this widow with child. He had not waited all these damned years, living like a monk, to put a bastard in the belly of a countess who did not dare meet him by the light of day. With a guttural grunt, he withdrew. The bliss was rolling up his spine. Blasting outward like fireworks in a dark sky. Nothingness, and then a glorious burst of brilliance and light. Gripping himself hard, Wolf spent on her mound, painting the pouting, red lips with his seed.

And he would be a liar if he said the sight of her, drenched in his mettle, breathless and dazed with passion on The Sinner's Palace's prized desk, did not fill him with a possessive sense of pride. It was primitive and raw, and he ought to be ashamed for thinking like a beast, but perhaps that was who he was.

Gradually, his sense of honor returned to him. He kissed her again, slowly and tenderly, before tucking himself back inside his trousers. And then, he extracted a handkerchief and cleaned her before reluctantly dropping her gown and petticoats, covering the sight of her long, stocking-clad legs.

Reality intruded, along with the reminder her time here was limited, and growing shorter with each passing second. Now that the haze of desire that had been clouding his mind was lifted, rational thought returned. He didn't dare fool himself into believing she had risked all in coming here merely for his sake. There had to be another reason. And likely, it was the one that had first brought her here days ago: her missing half brother.

"Now then," he said into the silence that had fallen between them. "Suppose you tell me why you've come."

## CHAPTER 10

*P*ortia sat opposite Wolf in a small, private dining room at The Sinner's Palace, her body still tingling in all the forbidden places he had brought her to life, and watched as he calmly filled a plate with those big, callused hands. He was capable of such gentleness. It was almost difficult to believe a man of his size could be so tender. That he would bring her to the heights of pleasure and then tend to her as he had done in the aftermath of their lovemaking.

She had been dazed, limp, and sated in the wake of their frenetic passion, words beyond her. And yet, Wolf had maintained the presence of mind to sense there had been another reason for her call upon him. He had not been wrong. But then, before she had been able to reply, he had asked her whether or not she had dined at her ball.

The answer was that she had not. Of course she hadn't. Sneaking away with the approval of her friend the Duchess of Montrose—and the use of Hattie's unmarked carriage—had meant that Portia had foregone the customary refreshments offered at the ball, along with the endless quadrilles and waltzes. The dances she did not particularly mind missing. Her quietly growling stomach, however, reminded her that sustenance would not be remiss.

She pressed a discreet hand to her midriff when he leaned nearer to deposit the plate before her. It was laden with a meat pie bearing a rich, flaky crust, some hothouse fruits, and vegetables in an herb-scented butter sauce. "Thank you."

"Wine?" he asked, already pouring her a glass.

"Yes, please." She accepted the offering from him, their fingers brushing and sending a new sense of awareness streaking through her. "You need not wait upon me, you know. I am perfectly capable of doing for myself."

"Of course you are, Countess." He sent her a charming grin and a wink. "But that doesn't mean I don't like doing for you."

He *liked* taking care of her. Her heart warmed.

Portia took a sip of her wine, surprised to note it was quite fine, and attempted to banish all the foolish warmth and tender feelings attempting to overwhelm her where Wolf Sutton was concerned. "The wine is as delicious as the meal looks."

Although she had not intended to offer insult with her observation, the moment the words left her, she understood how they must sound to him.

He raised a brow. "Believe it or not, we know what tastes delicious here in the East End just as well as the nobs in Mayfair."

She winced. "I did not mean to suggest otherwise."

He raised his own glass in mock salute. "No harm done, love. Now, eat your meat pie and tell me what brings you to The Sinner's Palace. Aside from my charming self, that is."

Guilt lanced her at his astute observation. "Please understand that I took a great risk in coming to you tonight, and it was one I could not justify if it were solely for my own gain."

He nodded, the teasing air fleeing his handsome countenance, leaving him looking uncharacteristically grim. "I understand your selflessness, Countess. What can I do for you?"

She took another hesitant sip of wine, needing to fortify herself, for every part of her loathed the realization she might have hurt him with her words. "I received another note from my half brother's mother a few days ago. She requested one hundred pounds. She requires the funds to help Avery, as she claimed."

"Naturally, you suspect her of lying," Wolf guessed, scooping up a forkful of meat pie from his own plate.

Her stomach rumbled again, so she gave in, allowing herself a bite of the flavorful, savory dish before continuing. "I do. Avery's mother is…a less-than-honorable woman. She was my father's mistress when my half brother was born, and she was one of London's most famed actresses at the time. Unfortunately, her obsession with drink and opium led her down a path to ruin. I have long feared she took my brother with her."

Wolf nodded. "She wouldn't be the first, and Christ knows she won't be the last."

Portia had seen Mrs. Courteney on more than one occasion in her youth, and always she had been struck by the other woman's arresting beauty and magnificent presence. It was a far cry from the destitute, haggard woman who had come calling to Portia's town house.

"When she and my father parted ways, it was not pleasant for her. I do think she loved him, in her own way," Portia said thoughtfully. "Or at least as much as Mrs. Courteney could love anyone other than herself. But then, Father was little different. I believe he loved her as well as he could have anyone. Either way, it is more than apparent that Mrs.

Courteney has suffered in the intervening years. She appeared to be inebriated when she paid me a visit."

Father's contentious marriage with Mother had led him to flagrantly disregard her wishes and propriety both by bringing his paramour of the moment to wherever it was that Mother was in residence. He had flaunted them, Portia suspected, with the desire to hurt her mother. But Mother had remained impervious and cold, unaffected by the appearance of each woman at her door. Mrs. Courteney, however, had been different from the others. Father had fancied himself in love with her. So much so that when the famed Mrs. Courteney had given birth to his illegitimate son, he had allowed Avery to live with and be raised side by side with his legitimate children.

For a time.

Wolf took a sip from his wine, and she found herself watching him, captivated, wishing for a wild moment that they were sharing an intimate dinner somewhere else. That she would not have to leave him in less than half an hour's time but that instead, she could linger, basking in his presence. She was briefly fascinated by the dip of his pronounced Adam's apple as he swallowed.

"You ain't going to give this Mrs. Courteney the blunt, I trust?" he asked, tearing her attention back to the discussion at hand.

"No." Granville would take note of a missing sum that large, without explanation. But there was no need to elaborate. "However, I was hoping you might have some advice for me."

It was strange to think that in the span of the few days since she had known him that Wolf Sutton would become someone she trusted with not only her body but her secrets. And yet, there it was. She *did* trust him. And not because she had no one else to whom she could turn. She had friends and acquaintances aplenty. Rather, it was because of Wolf himself. Being with him felt...natural and easy. She knew, to her core, that he was a good man. An honorable one.

Perhaps it took years of knowing the other variety of gentleman to understand.

"Advice," he repeated, his hazel stare narrowing in contemplation. "Aye, I'm happy to give it, and any help you'll be needing. Tell me what's troubling you."

She considered how to phrase her request. Since the thought had first occurred to her several days before when she had been perusing her correspondence, she had played out this scene in her mind repeatedly. And still, she had not reached a conclusion on how best to ask this man for his aid without revealing the full story to him.

"I would still like to find my half brother Avery," she began slowly, for that much was true, despite Granville's threats, and it did not disclose information that would entangle Wolf in her troubles. "I need to conduct the search very discreetly, however. No one must be aware of my involvement. The only connection I have to Avery is his mother, and I have no notion of where to begin."

Wolf tilted his head, considering her. "You were originally told he was working at The Sinner's Palace, yes?"

"His mother suggested he was. I should have known better than to trust her then, but had I not done so..." Her words trailed off as she realized what she had been about to say.

Far more than she could afford to divulge.

"If you had not done so, then you never would have met me," Wolf finished for her.

"No," she agreed quietly. "I would not have."

He surprised her by reaching across the table and settling his hand over hers. "I'm glad you trusted her long enough for it to lead you to me, Countess."

She told herself that she should withdraw from his touch. She admonished herself that this was the last time she dared to steal away and be alone with Wolf Sutton. This had to be their farewell.

But she could not pull away. Instead, she stroked the edge of his palm with her thumb, grateful she had met him. Thankful for his presence, his comforting touch. For *him*, full stop.

With her free hand, she reached for her wine, and then took a quick, fortifying sip. "I am glad, too."

"This half brother of yours," Wolf said, his hand lingering over hers. "What is his surname? Is it the same as the mother's, Courteney?"

"No," she said. "Courteney is the name of a more recent husband or protector of hers, I believe. Avery's surname is Tierney."

Wolf stiffened, the hand atop hers going still. "Tierney?"

She searched his hazel gaze, trying to fathom the reason for his sudden, abrupt change of demeanor. "Does the name mean something to you? Has an Avery Tierney ever been in your employ?"

He shook his head slowly. "I don't know of an Avery Tierney. But I do know of a cove named Archer Tierney."

Hope rose, despite the first name being different. "Do you know him? I have not seen Avery in years, but he has dark hair similar to mine. I expect him to be tall as our father was. His eyes are green as well."

His jaw hardened. "I'm sorry, love. I haven't seen him, so I can't say. But my brother Hart has."

Could it be that she was closer to finding her brother after all, despite the years and Mrs. Courteney's unreliability?

She slid her hand from beneath Wolf's and clutched it,

attempting to temper her excitement and yet failing. "You will ask him, then? For me?"

"Don't get yourself too excited. Even if he does share the same hair and eyes, it ain't enough to mean he's your brother. And even if he were..." Wolf paused, as if he were reluctant to finish his thought.

"If he were?" she prodded, desperate to know, overwhelmed with the possibility she could find Avery after all, and that he was indeed somehow connected to the world of The Sinner's Palace.

"He ain't a good man, Archer Tierney," Wolf warned solemnly. "Not the sort of cove you'd be wanting to know."

If Avery was indeed calling himself Archer Tierney now, she could only begin to imagine the reason. Had he been desperate to escape his mother's clutches? Had Mrs. Courteney ever truly known where Avery was? And just what manner of man was Archer Tierney, for Wolf to make him sound like such a desperate villain?

Her heart tripped over itself in eagerness, along with her thoughts. It required all the effort she possessed to calm them and make sense of the wild musings. "Still, you will ask your brother for me, won't you? Perhaps even arrange a meeting with this Archer Tierney fellow, so that I might speak with him."

Granville's fury would know no bounds were he ever to discover such duplicity on her behalf.

"I'll do what I can, but I make no promises," Wolf told her, his voice grim as his expression. "Tierney has disappeared."

The incipient optimism withered like a rose in winter. "Disappeared?"

"Aye." He gave another tense nod. "We've been seeking the rogue for a different reason. He's a ruthless moneylender, and he's involved one of my brothers in bad business of some sort. We ain't certain what just yet. It may take us some time to find him again."

"I have time." She had nothing *but* time. An endless, lonely expanse of it awaiting her. Speaking of which, she likely needed to return to the ball. "It would mean a great deal to me if you would let me know if you are able to find him, Wolf."

"Is that all that would mean a great deal to you, Countess?" he asked, sliding his hand away from hers at last as a new coolness came over his manner.

"No," she admitted, despite every intention otherwise. "You do as well. But you know I cannot…"

"And yet, you did." He gestured in the direction of the office they had so recently despoiled. "*We* did."

Again. Yes, she had. She was weak for him. So very weak. But she had to be strong. Much, much stronger. For Edwin's sake.

"I must take care," she managed quietly. "For my son."

"Aye, the lad must come first." The bitterness had fled Wolf's countenance at the mentioning of Edwin. "I understand. You're a good mother, Portia. A good sister, too."

His words sent another sharp stab of longing through her. Not desire this time, but rather, a longing to be free. Free to be with Wolf as she wished, without fear of discovery and the ramifications that would inevitably come if Granville discovered what she was doing.

"Thank you," she managed past a prick of rising tears. "You are kind to say so."

He gave her a crooked grin. "I'm not kind, love. I'm greedy. I want more of you, even though I know I can't 'ave you."

The missing *h* so noticeable in his speech told her, even more than his words, that Wolf meant what he was saying. When his customary polish slipped, his emotions were involved. Though whether the emotion was displeasure, desire, or something else entirely, she could not say.

"I wish it could be different," she murmured, breaking his steadfast gaze to glance down at the half-consumed plate of food he had laid before her. The hunger that had initially been plaguing her was gone, chased by the dismal knowledge that this would be the last time she was alone with Wolf thus. "But it cannot be. If you are able to find Archer Tierney, please send a note to my friend, the Duchess of Montrose, instead of to me."

Hattie had told her she would be pleased to receive correspondence on her behalf when Portia had managed to relay a portion of her tale to her friend earlier that evening. And Portia had to agree that her friend was right; messages from Wolf were best sent elsewhere. The duchess was aware of Granville's control over Portia's life, though Portia had not dared share her shame with anyone else.

Only Wolf knew she had been done violence.

He merely did not know who, and nor would he ever find out. Because he was not meant to become entangled in her sordid affairs. She would face her brother as she had been doing since Blakewell's death: on her own.

"The Duchess of Montrose, eh?" Wolf frowned, stroking his jaw.

"Yes," she said firmly, adding Hattie's direction. Severing ties with him was necessary, and yet she loathed it with the ferocity of a thousand burning suns. She hesitated, wishing she could linger, but knowing she did not dare. With a sigh, she continued. "And now, I really must return to the ball before my absence is noted."

Wolf raised a dark brow. "Of course you must. I'll be escorting you to your carriage, Countess."

Naturally. She already knew him well enough to understand that Wolf Sutton was a fiercely protective man, and those instincts seemed to have extended to herself almost from the first. There was no need to offer argument on the matter; he would not hear it. And she found herself grateful. She had not realized just how very wearying fighting all her battles alone had been until he had offered to take up the cudgels for her. Pity it was an offer she was destined to refuse.

But this, his accompaniment to the carriage, she could allow.

"Thank you, Wolf." She would don her veil and in an unmarked carriage, no one would be the wiser that it was the widowed Countess of Blakewell who had been alone in a gaming hell.

Granville would never learn of her secrets. And if she could find her lost brother at last? Well, she would consider herself fortunate indeed for crossing paths with the man before her.

She rose, a heaviness in her breast, and he did as well, offering her his arm. Portia accepted it in silence, wishing for the hundredth time that her circumstances were different. Knowing there was nothing to be done.

## CHAPTER 11

"What are the bloody odds?" Wolf grumbled, mostly to himself but ostensibly to the entire carriage, which—he was ashamed to admit—he'd forgotten for a moment included his sister.

His mind was thicker than mud. Difficult to tell a notion from an inkling. And all because of *her*. Portia. Meanwhile, he'd been tasked with playing the damned chaperone to the youngest in the Sutton clan yet again, a position to which he was wholly unsuited on the best of days and desperately unqualified for on the worst.

"That you'd find yourself in love with Archer Tierney's sister?" Lily asked as their carriage swayed through the narrow rookeries lanes that were as foul smelling and rough as they were familiar.

He sent his sister a ferocious scowl and drummed his fingers on his knee, wishing they had already arrived at their destination and that he had not confided in his sister earlier that morning at breakfast. Telling Lily about Portia had not been his intention, but he'd been deuced confused about what to do with the possibility she was Archer Tierney's half sister. And he hadn't wished to go to his brothers with the tale just yet; they would never allow him to hear the end of it.

"Here now, Lil," he said with a glower. "No one said a damned thing about *love*."

The word was difficult to say. It seemed to stick to his tongue like raw honey. And it filled him with a queer sensation. It made his chest swell and his head ache. He was not *in love* with anyone, curse it. Lydia had cured him of that notion.

Had she not?

"You needn't say it explicitly," his sister said calmly, stroking her gloved hand over the fur of the orange cat which was curled on her lap. "You have spent the entirety of the drive fretting over your countess—"

"She ain't mine," he interrupted, hating himself for the bitterness in his voice. But Portia had made it more than apparent he had no claims upon her.

Although he had offered her his help in not just finding her half brother but also protecting her from whatever bastard in her life had struck her, she had only accepted the former rather than the latter. But even so, he had to use a duchess he did not know and had never met as the conduit for his communication with Portia, as she had requested. It set his teeth on edge.

"Archer Tierney's sister, then," Lily said.

"Half sister," he corrected, still frowning, "and we don't know if Archer Tierney and Avery Tierney are the same cove."

"One syllable's difference," Lily drawled, patting the cat's head.

The feline gazed up at her in adoring fashion.

"Where did you find that damned cat?" he demanded, feeling vexed with his sister. With the orange-furred creature. With Portia.

Most of all, with himself.

"Behind The Sinner's Palace," his sister said calmly. "He was mewing quite loudly, but he was not readily seen. I searched for him everywhere, until I finally spied him hiding beneath a cart. The poor darling was terribly thin. I fed him some chicken and we have been friends ever since."

Why was he not surprised his sister had befriended a stray cat?

And why was said cat currently riding with them in this bloody carriage?

"Cats make me sneeze," he said, which wasn't true.

But the orange creature was purring so loudly that the hum traveled above the familiar sounds of the road. It was nettling for someone in this carriage to be so contented when he was in such turmoil. Even if that someone happened to be beast rather than mortal.

"Sir Bellingham shall take that into consideration." Lily rubbed the cat beneath its chin as she addressed it instead of Wolf. "Won't you, my little darling lad?"

"Sir Bellingham?" Wolf adjusted his hat, his eyes narrowing on his sister. "Never say you named the cat after Bellingham and Co.?"

"And what if I did?" Lily adjusted the cat on her lap, giving him a stubborn look he recognized all too well. "I like to shop there, and its owner is a bit of a stray himself."

Wolf flicked the brim of his hat in idle irritation, snapping it with his forefinger. "The owner, you say? And how are you acquainted with the high and lofty Mr. Bellingham?"

A flush quickly covered his sister's cheeks, and her gaze dipped back to the cat. "We are not acquainted. Not at all."

He detected guilt in her tone.

It felt better to divert his attention to his sister rather than bedevil himself with his own woes.

"Do not lie to me, Lily Sutton," he said, tapping the toe of her shoe with his boot. "Why is it you insist on shopping at that silly bleeding place with all the nobs? All of them looking down their aristocratic noses at you."

"Do you mean the silly bleeding place where you pretended you were married to your countess and had poor Mr. Smythe bring you all the gloves and lace as if you intended to buy it all?"

*Well, Christ.* How the devil did Lily know about *that*? His ears went hot, and he was damned thankful for the brim of his fine hat to cover them.

Eying his sister, he scrubbed his jaw with a gloved hand. "And what do you care to tell me about all the fans and slippers and lace and hats you've been keeping in your attic room?"

Her color heightened, her discomfiture at his question more than apparent as she clutched the cat a bit tighter to her chest. "Wolf Sutton, have you intruded upon my private room?"

Aye, he had done. Because he had been worried about her the day she had not attended the meeting along with the rest of their siblings. And because most of their family—save Loge, of course—was busy chasing after their own spouses and future spouses. Which left Wolf to do everyone else's bidding. Including invading Lily's room and finding it stuffed to the rafters with gewgaws.

"I was looking for you," he said truthfully. "You were missing, if you will recall."

Her nostrils flared. "I was at the foundling hospital."

Which was where they were going now. The foundling hospital had become a cause for Lily. But going there had also recently nearly managed to see her robbed.

"So you say," he allowed.

"Yes," Lily agreed cheerfully. "Just as *you* say you are not in love with your countess."

The blasted conniving little...

"She ain't my countess," he reminded his sister, glowering again.

Lily simply smiled and carried on petting her cat. *Sir Bellingham!* What a mutton-headed name for a goddamn feline. And the incessant, pleased purring the creature was continuing to emit, it was maddening. Why was the cat so bloody happy?

"Of course she is not," Lily said lightly.

"She ain't," he repeated, more firmly this time.

"But if she *is* Archer Tierney's sister, and if you *are* in love with her, and Archer Tierney *has* managed to involve our brother in something insidious and dangerous, then being in love with his sister is going to put you to your trumps, ain't it?" Lily asked shrewdly.

*Christ.*

"Forget everything I told you," Wolf grumbled, wondering why the devil he had confided in his vexing younger sister anyway.

"Perhaps I will, if you forget about what you saw in my room," Lily countered.

Though she was the youngest, she was certainly the most cutthroat of all the Sutton siblings.

"I'll not be bribed, Lil."

His sister simply shrugged, looking rather smug.

He glared at her. "I'm not in love with the Countess of Blakewell. Lydia's betrayal has cured me of the notion of loving anyone."

"Lydia was a foolish girl who likely regrets choosing to become Mr. Anthony Drummond's mistress over being your wife every day," his sister said.

Once, the mere mentioning of Drummond would have been enough to have his resentment soaring. But time had intervened, cooling his ire. The promises Lydia had made to

Wolf and the love she had sworn she felt for him had died a swift death when she had been offered *carte blanche* by a wealthier cove. Drummond's offer for Lydia to be his mistress had been far more lucrative to Lydia than wedding a mere partial owner of what had then been a struggling gaming hell. In the years since he had been a green, eighteen-year-old lad who'd thought himself in love with Lydia, The Sinner's Palace had grown far more successful.

He had begged Lydia to choose him that day. And she had told him she had made her decision.

*I can't choose you*, she'd said. *Drummond has promised me so much more than your love can buy.*

Wolf had thrown himself into the only constants in his life ever since: his family and their gaming hell.

"I don't suppose I'll ever know whether or not she had any regrets," he mused, startled to realize he felt nothing when he thought about it now.

Whether or not Lydia wished she had accepted his proposal instead of becoming Drummond's doxy, it had ceased to matter some time ago.

"Do you still wish she had married you?" Lily asked, astute as ever.

"No." The admission left him feeling lighter. *Freer.*

"What happened with Lydia was a long time ago. You were a different man then." Lily scratched the feline's head. "You are not the same, and neither is your heart."

She was not wrong, this vexing sister of his.

He frowned some more, wondering when Lily had grown so blasted wise. "I suppose it ain't."

Lily beamed. "You see? You *are* in love with Lady Blakewell. You only required a bit of aid in seeing it."

Absently, he flattened his palm over his chest, rubbing the space above his heart as he considered his sister's words. "How can you love someone you've only just met?"

It made no sense.

He did not want to believe it.

And yet…

He felt closer to Portia than he had ever felt to another. He could not deny that. The connection they shared was rare and unique, difficult to understand, but running beneath the surface of their every interaction just the same.

"Your heart recognizes itself," Lily said softly, sadly. "Regardless of what your rational mind wants, sometimes."

His brows snapped together as he considered his sister. "What do you know about hearts and love?"

"Precious little." The smile she sent him was melancholy. "I do read books."

He was not certain he believed her response. The carriage came to a halt, however, meaning they had reached their destination. As if protesting the abrupt sway of the conveyance, the cat delivered a loud mew.

"You never did say why you're bringing the bloody cat to the foundling hospital," he pointed out, curious.

His sister always had a reason for doing what she did, even if it was a mad one. Lily was…well, *Lily*. That was the best way to describe her, and for those who knew her, it summed everything up quite tidily. Her name was its own adjective.

"The children need more happiness," she said, shrugging a shoulder as she cradled Sir Bellingham to her bodice. "I tried to secure some toys for them, but I was unsuccessful."

"More happiness," he repeated, seeing the wisdom in his sister's words. "Ain't that what we all need?"

"If your happiness is to be found with the Countess of Blakewell, then you ought to pursue it," Lily said as she gave the cat another scratch behind his ears. "Pursue it, and her."

If only it were as simple as she made it sound.

But it wasn't. Everything with Portia was complicated. Challenging.

*Worth it.*

He banished the inner voice and cleared his throat. "You'll be wanting to hold tight to the creature so it doesn't escape and get trampled beneath the wheels of a passing carriage."

Lily pursed her lips, giving him a look he recognized. "And how do you suppose I have been caring for Sir Bellingham all this time without your intervention, brother?"

The carriage door opened, saving him from having to answer.

Shaking his head, Wolf rose from the bench seat. "You've a sharp tongue, sister."

He descended from the carriage and turned to help her disembark as well. Since her hands were already full of orange fur, he settled his hand on her elbow. He needn't have bothered. Lily was as light on the old dew beaters as a bird.

And so it was a surprise when she took a few steps, still clutching the cat in her arms, and stumbled to a stop, nearly spilling to the pavements. Wolf was there, catching her, keeping her steady. But her gaze was trained upon another carriage, which had already arrived prior to theirs.

"Tarquin?" she asked, almost to herself.

Wolf's suspicions, already heightened, were on guard. "What is amiss, Lil?"

Blinking, she shook herself and offered him a smile that was, he thought, falsely bright. "Nothing, of course. Let us go and see to the children, shall we?"

Wolf did not think he was incorrect. Something was indeed wrong. His youngest sister, who had such worldly advice to impart to him concerning love and the heart, was clearly embroiled in some manner of romantic troubles herself.

But how?

And with whom?

It was yet another mystery in a sea of them, for it seemed that the most important women in his life were determined to keep their secrets to themselves rather than confiding in him. And Wolf did not like it. Not one goddamned whit.

"Aye, let's see to the children," he said smoothly, guiding Lily toward the entrance of the unassuming foundling hospital. "And to this Tarquin, whomever the devil he may be."

But as they ascended the front walk, he found himself not just thinking of the mysterious gentleman who appeared to be plaguing his sister, nor solely about the children within, but rather about Portia and her son. About his heart, recognizing itself. And then about how soon he could see her again. There were ways. He would find them.

He was a bloody fool.

The worst sort.

~

Portia was a fool.

A reckless, silly, selfish fool.

Because all she could think about was Wolf.

Which was why, when the summons finally arrived from the Duchess of Montrose, Portia bundled herself into her carriage with the haste of a lady who had Cerberus on her heels, and practically ran to see Hattie. It wasn't Hattie awaiting her in her friend's salon, however. The man standing at the window, his back to her, was tall, broad-shouldered, and undeniably *him*.

"Wolf," she said, rushing to him before the door had even closed behind her.

He opened his arms as if it were the most natural reaction in the world, for her to come hurtling toward him as if she were a ball shot from a cannon. And she didn't falter in her stride until she was where she had longed to be ever since she had last reluctantly left that position: tucked against his chest. His musky, citrus scent enveloped her, at once familiar and alluring. She wrapped her arms around him, holding him tight.

Days had passed since she had last dared to venture to The Sinner's Palace.

And she had missed him.

"I missed you, Countess," he murmured, his words an echo of her own feelings.

She tipped her head back to feast on the sight of him, the strong blades of his cheekbones, the finely sculpted mouth, the slash of his nose, his stubborn jaw. "What are you doing here? Hattie's invitation made no mention of you."

"Fortunately, your duchess is acquainted with my brother Jasper's wife. Lady Octavia was able to vouch for me. Her Grace is otherwise occupied for the moment, but she was kind enough to allow us the use of this salon."

Portia resisted the urge to press her lips to Wolf's, for she did not suppose her friend intended them to use her salon for wicked purposes. Instead, she cupped his cheek, relishing the reassuring warmth of him.

"It is reckless of us to meet."

But she was glad he had managed to involve Hattie in his scheming. She would not deny it. Her heart was overjoyed to see him. And her body was overjoyed to have his so temptingly near.

"I trust the Duchess of Montrose is not the scoundrel responsible for the bruise on your cheek," he said solemnly, his gaze searching her countenance.

She supposed he was looking for further injuries. However, her brother had been too busy with other duties to pay her a call, and she had ventured to a sedate supper with his wife which had been blessedly uneventful, unattended by

Granville who had been at his club instead. She had not minded the reprieve. He did not often resort to violence, but knowing he was capable of it did not render his interviews particularly comforting.

"No," she answered Wolf quietly. "She is not."

He traced the backs of his fingers over her cheek in a caress that was so tender, her knees trembled.

"Will you tell me who is?" he asked.

She should have anticipated the question, she knew. But speaking of her brother, and the ugly, stinging slap he had delivered to her, was the last thing she wished to do when Wolf was within reach after so many days of agonizing waiting.

"Please do not ask it of me." She bit her lip to stave off the sting of tears.

He shook his head, his nostrils flaring. "I wish you would allow me to help you. I would give the bastard the thrashing he so richly deserves."

If only her problems could be solved by Wolf squaring off against Granville. She knew who would emerge the victor; without question, it would be Wolf, whose size and muscled physique would overpower Granville's claret-induced paunch any day. But all that such a meeting would accomplish was Wolf being sent away to one of London's vile prisons and Granville taking Edwin from Portia for good.

No, her position was untenable at best and hopeless at worst. Nothing could be changed.

She wetted her suddenly dry lips, deciding to change the subject. "What brings you here? Have you found Avery?"

Wolf's jaw hardened, his displeasure at her avoidance apparent. But he continued to hold her as gently as before, as if she were fashioned of glass. "Nothing is certain yet, but I needed to see you again. To hold you again."

His words made that last sliver of ice inside her melt.

But she told herself it was for naught. There was no future for herself and Wolf Sutton. Her brother would vanquish every chance she had for happiness. At least until Edwin was of age, and he was no longer subject to Granville's tyrannical rule. But years would pass before then.

Sadness crept over Portia. "I cannot do this with you."

"You cannot do what?" He raised a brow, cocking his head. "Stand here in the privacy of the Duchess of Montrose's salon? I see no one else about. Even the butler has gone, obliging cove that he is."

"Be with you," she clarified. "I cannot *be with you*, for it makes me want what I can never have."

"And why can't you have it?"

He was full of questions, and so handsome he made her ache with all the repressed longing she possessed. But she had to be strong.

Portia shook her head. "Because it is impossible."

"Plenty of things are impossible, Countess." The hand he had pressed to the small of her back moved in a slow caress up and down her spine, the heat of him traveling through the layers of her gown and undergarments, searing her in the best possible fashion. "Flying is impossible, unless you're a bloody bird. Swimming around the world is impossible, unless you're a damned fish, and even then, it ain't likely…"

She could not contain her smile. There was something about Wolf Sutton that was just so naturally charming. He was the sort of man she could fall in love with.

The realization was jarring.

"But I do not wish to fly," she said softly. "Nor swim around the world. Heavens, I cannot swim at all, and I certainly have no wings."

"Why is it impossible to be with me?" His fingers trailed over her jaw in the barest whisper of a touch. "You are here with me now."

Yes, she was.

And being with him felt like a dream.

A dream from which she would have to wake, and go on living the grim, passionless existence that had been her life these many years.

"This is finite," she explained grimly, reaching for his wrist and staying his hand when it touched her cheek. "It must end."

His jaw tensed, his hazel eyes flashing with an emotion she could not define.

"For now, you are here." His head dipped slightly, the parity in their heights rendering it easy for him to scarcely move and yet press his lips to her forehead in a sweetly unexpected kiss. "I am here. Let us think about the present rather than what happens when we part, aye?"

For a moment, she allowed her eyes to flutter closed. Permitted herself to imagine being with Wolf was not just fleeting but permanent. And savoring him, too. Savoring *them*. She liked who she was when she was with Wolf. Liked herself in a way she had not in longer than she could recall.

For so many years, Portia had buried herself in penance for her sins, marrying a man she did not love, being a faithful wife to him, maintaining a spotless reputation for the sake of her son. All so that she could shed the unwanted mantle of Lady Scandal she had received in her wild first Season. She had paid the price for her girlish longings, her impish curiosity, for trusting a gentleman who had proven himself not to be a gentleman at all. She had learned the most difficult lesson of all as a naïve lady who hadn't an inkling that a man who would profess to love her had also issued those same words to half a dozen other ladies, all of whom he had ruined by various means as well…

"Portia?"

Her eyes jolted open at Wolf's prod, and she fell into his hazel gaze. "Forgive me. My mind was drifting."

"To unpleasant places?" he guessed grimly.

"To places that make me understand myself," she answered honestly, and then wished she could retract the confession the moment it fled her.

For in her experience, vulnerability always heralded a betrayal. Whenever she had made herself weak to a man, he had exploited that weakness. Crushed her, heart and soul.

But Wolf was different. He was not like the other men in her life. The ones who had disappointed and hurt her. The men who hurt her still.

And he reminded her of just how different he was from them when he pressed his face to her neck and inhaled as if her scent were all he needed to fill his lungs. All he required.

"Have I told you I missed you?" he asked, his voice a deliciously low growl that teased her senses.

An ache began, the sort she knew could not be assuaged when they had only a few stolen moments in her friend's formal salon. But she smiled at his words just the same.

"You have. But you may say it again if you like."

"I missed you." He rubbed his cheek against hers, the prickle of his whiskers sending more heat to pool between her thighs.

"I missed you, too," she admitted at last, allowing herself to lower her defenses.

"You smell so fucking good."

His crude language startled a laugh from her. "I do?"

Wolf kissed her ear, making her shiver. "You do."

She suddenly became aware of his cock, thick and rigid, pressing against her lower belly. "Thank you."

She sounded breathless, even to her own ears. *Good heavens*, what was she doing, embracing him like this in Hattie's salon, where any moment her friend might walk through the door unannounced? It was the height of wanton disregard for propriety. And if Granville were to learn she had been paying a call to her friend at the same time as Wolf Sutton happened to also visit...

Another shudder went through her, uncontrollably.

Wolf must have sensed it, for he held her tighter. "Cold?" he asked.

"No."

"Ah." He kissed her ear again, his hand traveling up and down her back in that steady, reassuring caress. "No one shall know we were here together, love. Your friend the duchess is a square mort."

*A square mort.*

How was it that even his odd turns of phrase, the lack of polish his accent sometimes possessed, made her heart sing?

"She is indeed a square mort," she agreed. "Hattie is a true friend."

And she was beyond grateful for Hattie's steadfast nature, her willingness to overlook the oddity of Portia's requests. To offer the use of her carriage and her salon without batting an eyelash.

"Her husband ain't bad either," Wolf said. "I always thought dukes were arrogant arseholes, but I'm learning there are some who ain't."

She had a feeling that from Wolf Sutton, it was high praise.

Smiling, Portia kissed his whisker-studded cheek, relishing the abrasion on her lips. "The duke is a kind man, and he is hopelessly in love with Hattie. Most marriages are not founded on such a depth of emotion."

It was true. The Duke of Montrose was in love with his duchess, and it was plain for all to see. He worshipped Hattie, which was nothing less than Hattie deserved. And in return, Hattie loved her husband quite desperately.

"Your marriage was not founded on *a depth of emotion*, as you say?" Wolf asked, raising his head to study her once more.

And she could not shake the feeling that shrewd gaze of his saw far too much.

"It was not," she agreed simply. "Lord Blakewell was not a cruel man, but ours was... Well, suffice it to say that it was not a love match."

Far from it.

"He did not mistreat you?"

Wolf's question took her by surprise. Stunned her, for it brought along with it an astonishing realization.

Wolf Sutton *cared* about her. He cared about her past. It was almost too much to fathom.

"He was...kind," she said, lacking for a better descriptor. "He was thirty years my senior, and he possessed some notions I did not agree with, but he cared for me in a time when I very much needed it, and I shall forever be thankful for his generosity."

Speaking about Blakewell—her past—with Wolf, a man who could never be her future, felt odd. But she also wanted to tell him. Speaking about her marriage with the earl, even as she withheld a great portion of the true story, was remarkably freeing. It was as if a weight she had not known was there had been suddenly lifted from her chest.

She could breathe again.

"Trust me, love, his marrying you didn't have a bleeding thing to do with generosity," Wolf said wryly. "He was lucky to have had you as his wife."

Wolf's steadfast loyalty to her was equally heartening. He was a good man, and she knew it the way she knew the sun would rise again on the morrow. Instinctively. It simply just *was*.

"Thank you," she said.

"There's nothing between us that requires your thanks, Countess," he said gruffly, dropping a kiss to her temple and then releasing her.

As he stepped away, the withdrawal so sudden she almost cried out at the loss of his comforting strength, Portia took a step in retreat, reaching for the back of a nearby settee to steady herself. They stared at each other in silence for a few moments, a wealth of feeling passing between them, though no words were spoken.

There was so much she wanted to say.

*Everything.*

So many explanations on her tongue: her past, her mistakes, the way Blakewell had made a ruined girl into a countess, and how he had taken her under his protection, lending her his family's formidable reputation, claiming her son as his own… But then she had to remind herself that Wolf was very much still a stranger to her. A man she had only known for the span of less than a fortnight.

And she had made mistakes before.

Terrible ones.

She was still paying the price and living with the consequences of those mistakes, eight years later.

"There's something I must tell you, Portia," Wolf said, interrupting the war raging within her.

Her heart stumbled. "What is it?"

"It's Tierney." He scrubbed a hand over his jaw. "If he is indeed the brother you've been seeking, I have to warn you… whatever he's caught himself up in, it ain't a pretty spider's web."

*Avery.*

God, yes. How selfish was she, thinking only of herself, her own wants, desires, needs? She could not forget the reason she had met Wolf Sutton to begin with. Her sole reason for venturing to The Sinner's Palace had not been to fall in love with a handsome East End gaming hell owner, but to find her brother.

The thought sent her already stuttering heart plummeting to her slippers.

*Fall in love?*

Could it be? Had she?

Nay, there was no way she had fallen in love with Wolf Sutton. She scarcely knew him. He was… She was…

She was in love with Wolf Sutton.

In.

*Love.*

"Countess?" Wolf asked, his voice and his gaze equally concerned as they reached her. "Is something wrong?"

Everything. *Everything* was wrong. She was wrong. This was hopeless. *She* was hopeless. And utterly witless. She could not have fallen in love with a man who was the most unsuitable gentleman she knew, the sort of man Granville would never accept, the sort of man who would be more at home in the rookeries than the salon of a duchess that gleamed with gilt…

And yet, she had.

"Portia?"

She blinked. "I…no, forgive me. Nothing is wrong. I was merely upset by your suggestion that my brother could be involved in something that sounds as if it may be dangerous. *Is* it dangerous? And what do you suspect him to be engaged in? Surely not anything too nefarious, I hope."

Part of what she had just said was a blatant lie, but she was not willing to tell Wolf the truth. Not about to confess her mad, inconvenient, wholly astonishing feelings to him. Not going to reveal that her distraction had been owed to the abrupt realization that the emotions skittering through her were far more intense than desire. And that they all belonged to him.

That her heart was his.

"We don't know what Tierney is about, not for certain. He has been acting as a moneylender for the last few years." Wolf paused, shaking his head, his countenance grim. "But whatever he's doing, it ain't mere moneylending now. It's far more, and he's brought my brother into it, which is where it won't end well for him. We aim to bring our brother back to the family fold where he belongs."

If Avery was now calling himself Archer, and if what Wolf was telling Portia was to be believed, that meant that Avery was involved in something she could not even fully comprehend. Something so bad that Wolf was avoiding its utterance.

"Have you any notion of just what it may be that Archer Tierney is involved in?" she asked, needing to know and yet despising the possibility that she might discover the brother she loved was no longer a man she could care for.

Wolf shook his head. "Can't say just yet. We won't know until we have a talk with him, and the bastard is slipperier than water at the moment."

She nodded, understanding. But despite the inherent risks, despite the possibility of discovering Avery had become a man who she would no longer wish to know, she needed to find out whether or not he and Archer Tierney were the same, and no matter what he had done. "When you do speak with him, you will send me word?"

"Aye. Of course I will, Countess." His countenance was grim. "You'd best prepare yourself accordingly."

"I shall." And if Avery had changed his name and was involved in something dangerous, then she would have no choice but to accept it. Just as she had no choice but to accept that Granville had complete control over her present and future.

A subtle knock at the salon door intruded before either of them could say more.

"Portia?" called a familiar female voice from the opposite side of the door. "It is Hattie. May I enter?"

She understood why her friend was giving her the courtesy of a warning rather than simply entering a chamber within her own household. She knew that Portia and Wolf had other reasons for wishing to be alone, aside from the matter of Portia's missing half brother. Her cheeks went hot as she smoothed her gown and tentatively patted her hair, making certain nothing was out of place.

She cast a glance toward Wolf to make certain he was ready for Hattie's arrival, and he straightened his coat, nodding. They were as composed as they could possibly be after being in each other's arms.

Portia turned to the door. "Of course you may."

The door opened, and the duchess swept forward, lovely and elegant as ever in a pale gown that did its best to hide the swell of her belly, for Hattie was expecting another child. In her arms, she held a fat, white cat whose name was, of all things, Sir Toby Belch.

Wolf bowed. "Your Grace."

And heavens, how elegant and courtly he could be when he tried. He quite stole Portia's breath. But she forced herself to dip into a curtsy in deference to her friend, though she knew the formality an unnecessary one.

A welcoming smile crossed Hattie's lovely countenance. "You need not stand on ceremony with me. Goodness knows I am hardly an adherent to rules. Indeed, I can hardly tolerate them myself."

Her friend's unconventional nature was refreshing to Portia. Fortunately, being friends with a duchess, regardless of how little care she paid to society's strictures, was good enough for Granville. He encouraged her friendship with Hattie and never took issue with the calls Portia paid her.

"I reckon we have intruded upon your fine salon long

enough," Wolf said wryly. "Thank you, Duchess, for your generosity."

His words sent a fresh ache through Portia, a pang of a different sort.

Because parting ways was the last thing she wished to do, though she knew they must.

Hattie scratched Sir Toby's head. "You are more than welcome. I am always eager to aid friends, and Portia is a dear one."

"You know I feel the same," Portia said. "I am very grateful for your discretion."

Having a trusted friend she could rely upon was proving an immeasurable gift, especially since Hattie was willing to facilitate these clandestine meetings with Wolf.

"Whatever you need, my dear." Hattie smiled.

*If only.*

Portia knew that what she needed—truly needed—was not what she could have.

As if he sensed the direction of her thoughts, Wolf's gaze met hers. "I'll be in contact with you soon, Lady Blakewell. If you will excuse me, Your Grace, my lady. I must take my leave."

As she watched the man she loved walking away from her, Portia could not repress the miserable aching in her heart.

## CHAPTER 12

Wolf had a pistol tucked obligingly inside his coat, a blade hidden in his boot, two waiting carriages parked just out of sight, and three of his brothers flanking him on the street.

The time had finally come to confront Logan.

And, along with him, Archer Tierney.

"I'll draw my weapon first," Jasper said, keeping his voice low. "We need to keep Loge and Tierney separate. Wolf, you and Hart take Tierney into your carriage. Rafe and I will take Loge."

Aye, what they were about to do was a trifle…unconventional. They were kidnapping Loge and Archer Tierney. There was no other word for it, no better means of describing the plan they had arrived at together after they had discovered where Tierney and Loge were hiding. It was a tad ruthless. A mite criminal.

But necessary.

They weren't going to give Loge another chance to disappear again. And Tierney, well, he was coming along to explain what role he'd played in this bad business. Wolf had some questions to ask him of his own as well. Because if the bastard was indeed Portia's lost brother, then Christ. He'd have to contend with that.

But first, they were going to have to capture the scoundrel.

Fortunately, the men Jasper had been paying to find Tierney and Loge had not just discovered their new establishment inside a printer's shop. They had also taken note of the patterns of Loge and Tierney when they were coming and going.

"Loge should be leaving at any moment," Rafe added.

"Now," Jasper said urgently, before whistling to alert the first carriage to be at the ready.

As if on cue, a familiar figure strode past the narrow alleyway separating shops from one another. Moving quickly, Jasper and Rafe slipped behind Loge. Jasper grasped Logan's arm and withdrew his pistol, which he pressed to Logan's back. Because they had no wish to shoot their brother, Jasper's pistol bore no ammunition, but Loge didn't know that, and they knew he wouldn't accompany them without force. Rafe gripped Logan's other arm. The carriage rolled forward.

"Get into the carriage, Logan," Jasper commanded. "There ain't any other choice."

"What the hell are you doing?" Loge snarled. "You're dicked in the bloody nob if you think I'm going anywhere with you."

Jasper and Rafe ignored his protests, forcing him toward the carriage. Another loud whistle, and the carriage door opened to reveal Hugh, who leapt down and aided Jasper and Rafe. The struggle that ensued was ugly and brief. Thankfully, it ended with all four men in the carriage. Sleepy Tom cracked the whip, and they jolted down the road in the direction of The Sinner's Palace.

"They've taken him," Wolf said, unaware he'd been holding his breath as he watched the scene unfold until now.

There was no telling how long they would be able to hold Loge, especially if he realized Jasper's pistol didn't bear any bullets. But given the manner in which he'd disappeared when they'd found him the last time, they knew this was the only way to get him alone and hopefully force him to listen to reason. Whatever he was involved in with Tierney, they would help him to extricate himself. Family was family, and Suttons were nothing if not loyal.

"Thank Christ," Hart muttered at his side. "I didn't think they would get him to go."

"The pistol in the back helped," Wolf said grimly, for he hated that their brother had become so far removed from the family that it required a damned gun to force him to speak with them.

But they had tried. Hart had tried. And then Logan had disappeared again.

Now Tierney was next. Because Wolf didn't trust him one whit, and because they didn't share blood, he wasn't taking any chances. His pistol *was* loaded, as was Hart's. But they would have to wait. According to Jasper's men, Tierney and Loge never arrived or departed at the same time. Tierney would leave later, under cover of darkness.

A sudden flurry of commotion reached them, and Wolf realized the shouts were coming from the direction of the printer's shop.

"Damn it," Hart muttered. "They must have seen Jasper and Rafe taking Loge."

Wolf whistled for the other carriage, thinking they would need it in a hurry, whether to make their own escape or for Tierney, as had originally been planned. The carriage bearing Randall lurched forward.

But the undeniable barrel of a pistol being jammed into Wolf's own back made him freeze.

"Don't make a bloody move," ordered an icy voice behind him.

"Tierney," Hart spat, similarly stiff at Wolf's side.

Out of the periphery of his vision, Wolf took note of the pistol burrowed into his brother's coat. It would seem the wily bastard had a weapon trained upon each of them.

"Hell and damnation," Wolf muttered.

"Call off your carriage," Tierney snapped.

Wolf hesitated.

Tierney prodded him with the pistol. "I said call off your goddamn carriage. If you don't, I'll have my men shoot your bloody coachman."

He glanced to Hart.

"Do it," his brother said.

Wolf whistled again, then made a gesture to Sly Jack, the coachman, letting him know he wasn't to come. The driver nodded and proceeded past.

"Good choice, Sutton," Tierney growled. "Now then, the two of you will be coming with me."

They had no choice. It was either risk their own lives and that of their men or do as Tierney demanded. Since Jasper and Rafe had taken Loge, there was always the hope that Tierney would not do anything too rash. Wolf had no intention of dying tonight. He had far too much to live for.

Portia's lovely face flitted through his mind's eye.

And that included a woman who very well could be the half sister of the cove who had a pistol pressed to his spine.

~

PORTIA EXAMINED her son's pastel drawing, impressed with his work. It bore the rudimentary lines of a child's artistry to be certain, but there was something undeniably talented about the way he had depicted the vase of fresh hothouse flowers she had arranged earlier that morning. He had even captured some of the light streaming in through the windows, illuminating the petals with a crayon of Naples yellow. It was a pleasant diversion to spend time with Edwin, the perfect way to distract herself from the ever-present, inconvenient longing for Wolf that never ceased plaguing her.

"How wonderful!" she exclaimed. "You have perfectly captured the delphiniums and the lilies. I adore it, my love."

Edwin stared down at his drawing, frowning. "You adore it?"

"Of course." She smiled reassuringly. "You know how much I love all your sketches."

"I suppose you *must* love them," he said, stroking his chin as he considered his creation. "You are my mother."

That was true, of course, and it was rather alarmingly perceptive of her son to suppose it.

"Mothers are not required to love their sons' sketches," she pointed out.

Her own mother, for instance, had never taken interest in anything Portia had produced, whether it be embroidery or watercolors or music. But she did not add that eternally dismaying fact to her observation.

"Hmm," Edwin said, shrugging his shoulders before finally glancing up at her. "Uncle says pastel crayons ought to be left to women. He says that I am a gentleman and when I am a lord, I will have many duties far too great to allow time for such a feminine art."

Her nails curled into her palms at the mention of Granville. Naturally, her brother would have something oafish and insulting to say about Edwin's sketches. She forced her resentment to subside, however, for dwelling on her fury would do her no good.

She patted her son's back. "Lords are entitled to enjoy whatever pastime they wish, darling. Some may prefer to hunt, others to ride, some to make sketches. You need not always listen to your uncle."

*Because he is wrong.*

*Because he is a hateful tyrant who presumes to know better than everyone else.*

*Because he delights in crushing spirits, and he shall do his utmost to destroy yours as well.*

But she said none of those things, tucking all her warnings away instead. Portia was ever cognizant that her son could naively repeat some of her words of caution to her brother. And if that were to happen…

A shudder went through her.

No, that must never happen. The more she was able to shelter her son from the storm that was her elder brother, the better.

"Is Uncle the one who ruined your paper-hangings?" Edwin asked her, his pensive voice slicing through her own ruminations.

Shocking her.

"Of course not. Why would you think so?" She swallowed, the lie propelling itself swiftly.

She told herself it was for her son's sake, to shield him from the ugliness of the world for as long as possible. But she also knew she deceived everyone around her about her brother's violence because she was ashamed.

"Your inkwell was missing," her son said, holding her gaze with his own, so like hers. "You said the maids overset it, but how would it have gone onto the wall? Uncle paid me a call the same day."

Her son was clever.

Too clever.

And how she loathed lying to him.

"Why should you think it was Uncle?" she asked, attempting to understand his reasoning, deflecting his questions.

Had he overheard her arguing with Granville? Had her brother revealed something of their contentious relationship to her son?

"I heard one of the maids whispering about it," Edwin admitted, then looked down sheepishly. "I know I am not meant to eavesdrop, Mama. I did not intend to, truly. Are you angry with me?"

The maids were gossiping about her brother. The knowledge made her go cold.

"Of course I am not," she said. "But Edwin, it is important that you do not mention what you heard to Granville. He would be most displeased to learn of any untoward chatter concerning him. Do you understand?"

*Good heavens*, if Edwin were to go to her brother with such accusations, she had no doubt he would be furious. And she could not bear for her son to endure the brunt of Granville's wrath. Not now. Not ever. She would protect him as she always had, however she must. No price was too great to pay.

"I understand, Mama." Edwin looked up at her, his eyes searching for answers she had no wish for him to see. "It is true then, is it not?"

She closed her eyes for a moment, wrestling with her answer. If she revealed that Granville had indeed smashed her inkwell against her prized paper-hangings in a fit of pique, Edwin would likely have more questions she did not dare answer. But if she continued lying to him...

On a deep breath, she opened her eyes, holding her son's gaze. "It is true, yes. And that is why you must never repeat what you heard to your uncle. It is imperative that you do not displease him in any way."

"I know Uncle is not a kind man," her son startled her by confiding.

Her heart felt as if it were being constricted in her chest. "How?" she managed, her voice hoarse. "How do you know?"

If Granville had dared to strike her son...

"He never smiles," Edwin told her, his countenance grave. "And he speaks cruelly to the servants. After he visits, you are always sad. A nice man would not intentionally ruin the paper-hangings with ink. I would never do that to you, Mama."

*Thank God.* He had not struck Edwin. Relief washed over her, so profound and violent that her knees trembled.

"I know you would not do that to me, my darling boy." She held her arms open to him, and when Edwin moved forward, she folded him in her embrace. "You are a kind and wonderful lad, and I am ever so glad to be your mama."

"I am glad you are my mama, too," he said, holding her tightly.

She kissed his crown. "This shall be our secret, Edwin. We'll not speak of it again."

"Yes, Mama," he said dutifully. "I promise I'll not say a word to Uncle. But I do wish he would not be so mean."

She wished the same, and then some. Oh, how she wished she were free of this terrible situation. Free to live her life as she chose, free to love Wolf. But there was no escaping the provisions Blakewell had left in his will. Her husband had been well-intentioned, she knew, unaware of what her brother was capable of. He had believed it important for his son to have the guiding influence of a peer rather than relying upon Portia.

On account of her past.

And now, she was well and truly trapped, without hope of happiness. Not for herself, and not for her son.

"May I keep your sketch of the flowers?" she asked Edwin, attempting to change the subject to happier topics. "I would dearly love to see it framed and hung on my wall."

"Perhaps you might hang it over the ink stain," her son suggested.

"Excellent notion, Edwin." Smiling sadly, she kissed his crown again. "I shall do just that."

∼

"You are a publisher now, Tierney?" Hart asked, casting a glance around the room where their captor had brought them.

"I am whatever I need to be," Tierney said smoothly, the brace of pistols he was using to coerce them still firmly trained on Wolf and his brother. "And you are asking questions when you ought not, Sutton."

Wolf and Hart were seated in a room bearing printing equipment, the place pungent with the scents of ink and paper and machinery. Tierney's henchmen had closed in on them in the alleyway, swiftly divesting Hart and Wolf of their respective weapons. Not even their hidden blades had gone overlooked. Their hands were tied behind their backs, and Tierney presided over them, looming like a beast of hell.

"What do you intend to do with us?" Wolf demanded, cursing himself for being foolish enough to allow himself and Hart to get caught.

Now, they were at the mercy of a man who was, if rumor and his pistols were to be believed, a deadly villain. A villain who had somehow caught their brother Logan in his tangled, dangerous web.

At least Logan had been spirited away without incident. But Wolf did not like being without the means of defending himself. And he certainly did not like having his damned hands tied behind his back as he stared down the barrels of two pistols.

"I thought we could have a little patter between us," Tierney said. "Seeing as how you bloody Suttons are determined to haunt my business at every turn."

Wolf tried to maintain his composure, to keep Tierney talking to give himself and Hart time to attempt to free themselves. Behind his back, the knots at his wrist were already loosening. "And what is your business?"

"A bit of everything," Tierney responded coolly. "And my business ain't none of yours."

"Logan is our brother," Hart growled. "Everything about him is our business."

"Family is more than blood," Tierney said with a shrug. "I reckon he can decide on his own what pleases him and what doesn't."

Wolf seized the opportunity in the conversation. "What do you know of family, Tierney? I don't suppose you have any, do you? Or is it possible that you left your family the same way Logan left ours? That you changed your name and abandoned your sister?"

Something sharpened in the man's gaze, but it was the sole evidence of a response to Wolf's prodding queries.

Tierney blinked, remaining calm. "I've no notion of what you're speaking about. I don't have a sister."

"No? Odd, that. I've been told you've a sister named Portia and that you once called yourself Avery," he continued, daring to take the risk of angering a man who was threatening him with a pistol.

Because he had to.

For the sake of the woman he loved.

He wanted to get her the answers she deserved. *Floating hell*, he wanted to do so much more for her than that. He wanted to spend time with her that wasn't mere stolen, fleeting moments. Wanted to get to know her son. To take the lad under his wing. To make Portia his in every way.

He swallowed against a rising well of emotion, forcing himself to hold Tierney's stare.

"And who told you that?" Tierney asked, his jaw rigid.

Wolf had a suspicion the man was not as unaffected as he pretended.

"The lady herself," Wolf drawled, feigning his own lack of concern.

He had no wish to cause problems for Portia, but there was only one way to discover whether or not Tierney was truly her half brother. And that was by leading the man along. Archer Tierney wasn't the sort of cove to willingly offer information that might better be used to suit himself.

Tierney's eyes narrowed, and for the first time, it occurred to Wolf that they were the same shade of green as Portia's. He was also tall. Taller than Wolf by a hair.

"Why would a lady of noble breeding lower herself to consort with a rogue from the rookeries?" Tierney sneered.

*Ah.*

A surge of triumph went through Wolf, for the man had already taken the bait, and with such bloody ease, too.

He leaned forward in his chair, all while still attempting to work his bonds. "Nobody said anything about her being a nob now, did they, Tierney? I know I didn't." He turned to Hart. "Did you say anything about her being a fancy mort, brother?"

Hart shook his head slowly. "Can't say that I did."

"You implied it," Tierney countered, his nostrils flaring in irritation.

"I called her a lady," Wolf agreed. "It's more polite than referring to her as a wench. Wouldn't you agree?"

"Are you trying to vex me, Sutton?" Tierney asked coldly.

"Seems rather foolish when you've my pistol pointed at your heart, does it not?"

"If you intended to shoot us, you'd have done it by now," Hart said boldly.

And Wolf had to admit, he did not think his brother's bluster was wrong.

"I've shot men for lesser sins," Tierney said.

"I'm certain you have, but I doubt you'd chance the wrath of the Suttons raining down upon you." Behind his back, Wolf attempted to twist his right wrist, where the bonds had loosened. "Jasper would chop off your tallywags and feed them to his dogs while you watched."

Once more, Tierney's gaze narrowed. "Take care with your threats, Sutton. I wouldn't be issuing them, were I you."

"Well, you ain't me, and I'm bloody glad for that," Wolf countered.

"I'd prefer to not be staring down another cove's gun, hands tied behind my back," Tierney said, his tone smug.

*Not for long, if I have anything to say about it, you scoundrel.*

But Wolf kept that thought to himself, tamping it down along with the festering resentment.

"Let us move past this bleeding stalemate, Tierney," Hart interrupted. "Tell us what it is you want from us."

"That is simple." Tierney raised a brow. "I want you and the rest of your siblings to leave me alone. Stay the hell away from me, my businesses, and anyone who works for them. It ain't difficult, you'll find. You stay in your part of the rookeries where you belong. I'll stay in mine."

"This here shop looks like a step up from the rookeries to me," Hart observed.

And he was not wrong. The printer's shop was situated in an area that was dense with other merchants and stores. Almost respectable. At least, for a moneylender from the East End. However, if Tierney truly was the bastard son of a lord as Wolf increasingly suspected of the man, then it was a far cry from the life to which he would have been accustomed as Portia's half brother.

"I'm a businessman," Tierney growled. "It ain't any concern of yours where, what, or how."

"It is when you involve our brother," Wolf bit out.

Tierney sighed. "This grows tiresome. Your brother is old enough and smart enough to know where his loyalty ought to lie, and it ain't with your gaming hell. Accept it and forget about him."

"We can't do that," Hart denied.

"And your brother can't be controlled by you. I'm guessing that when your family grows weary of attempting to persuade him to return to your flock, they'll come to me offering a trade. Two in exchange for one. I'll still be getting the better end of the deal."

"Or Loge will return to our fold," Wolf argued. "Where he belongs."

Tierney smiled, though it was more feral than pleasant. "We'll be seeing that, won't we?"

"I suppose we will, *Avery*," he said pointedly.

The other man stiffened instantly. "That ain't my name."

"She's in trouble, you know," Wolf added, ignoring Tierney's denial. "If you are her brother, and if you ever cared a bloody damn for her, you'd be trying to protect her instead of hiding away like a louse."

"Trouble," Tierney repeated, his tone dark. "What sort?"

Apparently, Wolf had his attention now.

"Someone has been beating her," he ground out. "She'll not tell me who, or I would gladly thrash the bastard."

At his side, Hart was watching the conversation unfold with an interested gaze.

Wolf ignored him, for he was determined to get Portia

her answers, however he must. And it seemed that only Archer Tierney possessed them.

"You are sure about this?" Tierney demanded of Wolf.

He inclined his head. "I saw the bruising myself."

"Christ," Tierney muttered, then shook his head, as if clearing it of something unwanted. "It ain't any concern of mine if the wench is being beaten. Mayhap she deserved it."

The coldness in Tierney's eyes and voice, coupled with his suggestion Portia had deserved the abuse she had suffered, was enough to have Wolf surging from his chair. Unfortunately, his wrists were still bound too tightly for him to free himself, and Tierney's henchmen were quick to step in. It took three of them to fight Wolf back into his seat, and when he was lashed to the legs, he was panting, glowering at Tierney, ready to commit bloody murder.

"She didn't deserve it, you arsehole," he spat. "If Jasper doesn't kill you after this, I will."

"Wolf," Hart cautioned quietly at his side. "Calm yourself."

But he could not. His heart was galloping in his chest. He felt like a beast. Ready to rage and roar and tear anyone who dared hurt Portia limb from limb. If only he knew who had done it, he would.

Tierney, however, appeared unaffected by his outburst. Instead, he flicked a glance toward the men who were hastily knotting Wolf's and Hart's legs to the chairs. "That shall do, lads. I've a call to pay. Watch them until I return."

"Where are you going?" Wolf demanded. "You can't leave us here like this."

Tierney smiled again. "I regret to inform you that I can. Until later, gents."

With an abbreviated bow, he took his leave, still carrying a pistol in each hand.

"You had better hope that bastard ain't going to pay a call on your woman," Hart muttered.

Well, hell.

What a muddle.

It was entirely possible that was *exactly* where Tierney was going. Of course, finding Portia would mean he knew who she was and where she lived, that Tierney had at least remained aware of his sister from afar in the years since they had last seen each other. He had no way of knowing, just as he had no means of determining where Tierney was headed. Meanwhile, Wolf could do nothing but remain where he was, tied to a damned chair, incapable of doing anything to help or warn Portia.

He was a failure.

An utter, abject failure.

## CHAPTER 13

In her sitting room, Portia stared at the framed sketch Edwin had suggested they hang to cover the ink stain on her paper-hangings, unseeing. Before her, partially finished and awaiting her quill on the surface of her writing desk, was the letter she had been carefully drafting for Hattie. Because she could not be certain if Granville had tasked anyone with reading her correspondence, she had to refrain from mentioning any topic of greater concern than the weather or a desire to pay a call.

She was restless.

Days had passed.

Four more of them.

And still, not another word from Wolf.

Portia missed him desperately, but there was no hope for it. If he hadn't any news concerning Avery, then it was best that she not have any contact with him. She knew it, and yet that did not render the distance between them any more bearable.

A knock at the door intruded upon her troubled musings.

To her surprise, it was her butler.

"You have a visitor, my lady," he said, offering her the card of her unexpected guest.

Portia's heart nearly dropped to her slippers when there, on the salver, was the name Wolf had mentioned to her.

Mr. Archer Tierney.

*Avery.*

She swallowed against a rush of hope, attempting to maintain her composure. "Thank you, Riggs. You may see him in."

"Of course, Lady Blakewell," the butler replied before disappearing once again.

After he departed, she rose from her desk, agitated, hands trembling, stomach clenched in a knot. Avery had come to her at last. But Wolf had warned her he was dangerous. And Wolf had promised he would send word before arranging a meeting, should he determine Archer Tierney and Avery were indeed the same person.

But he was here. Archer Tierney—Avery—was here. Alone, and without Wolf.

Her emotions churned within her in a tangled mess as she realized that Granville would likely learn about this call. He would discover Avery had been here to see her, and when and if he did, no amount of explanation on Portia's behalf would mitigate her brother's rage. He would be merciless in his retaliation.

Would he take Edwin from her?

Panic gripped her so fiercely that she did not hear the door open. Scarcely understood Riggs announcing Mr. Tierney.

As if in a dream, she turned toward the threshold.

And instantly recognized her half brother.

There was no doubt in her mind that the tall, grim-looking man before her was the boy she remembered. The brother she had loved so dearly. The one who had rescued her from a tree. Who had helped her to bind the wing of a bird Granville's pet cat had injured. Who had read to her in the nursery.

"Thank you, Riggs," she managed to tell the butler, her lips numb.

Her heart numb, too.

Her gaze met Avery's, as green as her own. As green as she remembered. He still had the slight bump in his nose from when they were younger and he and Granville had been fighting at Hardesty Manor after Granville had pushed Portia into the lake. She'd been unable to swim, and Avery had jumped in after her, pulling her choking and coughing and terrified from the waters. He had likely saved her life. After he had been assured of her safety, he had been furious. Avery had pushed Granville. And their eldest brother had been older, stronger. Granville's fist had landed square upon Avery's nose...

She was scarcely aware of Riggs taking his leave, of the door closing.

"Avery," she said, half whisper, half plea.

It had to be him, the brother she loved.

"Archer," he corrected coolly, his entire demeanor frozen and stiff.

As if he felt nothing. As if he did not remember the bond they had shared. But she had not forgotten. She never would, nor could she. So many years had passed since they had last seen each other, but she recognized him. He still possessed the same wavy, mahogany hair, and he had grown into his shoulders and long legs. He was a tall, forbidding man now. No longer a lad.

"Brother," she said instead, for it was the title she preferred, if he refused to acknowledge his true name.

His lips tightened. "I'm not anyone you should know."

He had not denied their familial connection, at least. This heartened her, even if fear of Granville loomed.

"Why should I not?" she asked.

He issued a bitter chuckle. "All the reasons one might suppose. I am a scoundrel. A villain. A criminal. I kill. I steal. I lie. I do whatever I must to make myself rich."

She shook her head. "I do not believe you."

He shrugged. "Then don't. The choice is yours, my lady."

"I am your sister," she said, needing to hear him acknowledge their connection. Needing to be certain.

Why, she could not say. She had all the proof she needed in his presence here, the bend in his nose, his emerald eyes. His voice. It was the same, only lower. And his face was the same as she recalled, only he had grown into a man when the last time she had seen him, he had been very much a boy.

What had happened to that boy in the intervening years, to cause him to become so cold and jaded, so cynical?

"You would be wise not to claim me," he said, rather than denying her words.

And she knew for certain in her heart.

This was Avery before her.

"You are my brother," she said fervently.

The brother she had been searching for. The only brother who had loved her. Protected her. And the brother she loved in return. It did not matter what he had done, who he had become. She knew that now.

"Half brother," he countered coolly. "A bastard best cast to the wolves."

*Cast to the wolves. Half brother.*

He had acknowledged it, at least. Still, she knew little relief. For his response was leaving her with more questions than answers.

"What happened to you, Avery?" she whispered. "Where did you go?"

"Archer," he said again. "That is my name. It is who I am now."

"Archer," she agreed reluctantly, and only for his sake. "You disappeared."

"I was taken away, but it is immaterial now," he said shortly. "What happened occurred many years ago, and it is in the past, where it belongs."

"Taken away," she repeated, struggling to understand. "By whom? Your mother?"

"By yours," he snapped. "But never fear, the bitch who sired me was eager to be of service. Essentially, she sold me. The countess paid her a price, and she accepted, and I was taken away."

*Mother.*

Portia closed her eyes, reeling at the revelation. She should have known, of course. Her mother had never been kind to Avery. Indeed, she had made no effort to hide her resentment. Still, Portia had never supposed her mother had been behind the abrupt disappearance of her half brother. After all these years, learning it had been her mother and not her father or Mrs. Courteney as Portia had supposed came as a shock.

She opened her eyes again, needing to reassure herself that Avery was indeed in her sitting room. Standing before her after so long. "Where? Where did they take you?"

"No, my lady." Her half brother shook his head. "You ain't the one asking the questions here. I am. So tell me, who has been raising his fists to you?"

Portia felt the blood leach from her face. "No one."

A muscle twitched in her brother's jaw, an indication of how tightly he held himself. "Don't lie to me. I've come here for one reason, and that's to discover who dared to hurt you."

Wolf had told him.

Disappointment, hurt, shame, and fear collided.

"I do not know what you are implying," she lied.

Because lying was easier than admitting what she allowed—what she had no choice but to allow. It gave her control of a situation over which she had none.

"It was him," her brother said, lip curling in a sneer.

And he did not need to elaborate or offer a name. They both knew who her brother was speaking of.

*Granville.*

Portia did not want to cause any more problems for herself than Avery's visit would already produce. She had no choice, after all, but to live beneath the marquess's rule.

She took a deep breath. "I have no notion of what you are suggesting, but—"

"Stubble it," he interrupted, a snarl. "Don't lie to protect him."

The rage emanating from Avery—Archer, as he would have her think of him now—was palpable. She stared, stricken.

"Where is Wolf?" she asked him instead of confessing as he had demanded. "Why have you come to me? Surely he must have told you the difficulties you are inviting for me by calling upon me."

She was deflecting, it was true. But Portia had become quite adept at the art. Hiding her misery, prevaricating, distracting. Years of it.

"Wolf, is it?" Her brother's eyes narrowed. "Care to tell me how you're so familiar with Sutton?"

"He is my friend." Another lie. Wolf was far, far more. No mere word could capture him and what he was to her. "Not that it is any of your concern. You cannot reappear in my life after all these years and make demands of me."

He shrugged. "If you don't want to give me the answers I seek, I'll go to Granville. Is that what you want?"

The ice in her heart returned. "No. Please. You must not go to him."

Her brother's countenance changed, perhaps at the vehemence in her voice, softening. "I've been waiting to ruin him, Portia," he said, his tone gentling. "Tell me what power he has over you."

The dam inside her broke.

"My son," she admitted. "Blakewell named Granville as Edwin's guardian in his will. Granville has threatened to take my son from me if I do not abide by his rules. I have no choice but to do as he wishes, and he has been very firm in his disapproval of me attempting to find you."

"Christ," he spat. "He must love the power that gives him."

"Yes," she agreed quietly. "I expect he does."

"And he has done you violence," her brother repeated.

Her eyes closed and she inhaled, searching for the strength to confide in the stranger who was also somehow still her brother. How strange it was that he should have been missing from her life, only to return as if he had never been gone. He still wanted to protect her against Granville. This time, however, she could not let him.

"He has," she admitted at last. "But there is nothing that can be done. My circumstances are quite hopeless."

But the brother before her was not appeased by her words.

"That's where you're wrong, sister," he said grimly, his hands flexing at his sides. "There is always something that can be done. All I need is a bit of time, and I'll make certain that bastard never hurts you again."

With a curt bow, the brother she had spent years fruitlessly searching for turned and strode from her sitting room.

"Archer, please," she called after him. "Wait."

But he did not heed her.

And Portia knew what she needed to do. She had to get to

The Sinner's Palace with all haste so she could act before Archer did. She needed help, and there was only one man she trusted.

*Wolf.*

~

WOLF RETURNED to The Sinner's Palace with Hart, wearier than a traveler. Hours had passed since their ill-fated mission to bring Loge back into their ranks had begun. They'd failed miserably. Tierney had finally released them without a word of where he had gone or why. The man had been stony and cold and silent, save for the communication that they could leave—and without the return of their own weapons.

"He's gone back to Tierney," Jasper confirmed of Logan as the Sutton brothers reconvened in the office of their gaming hell. To protect their beloved sisters, they had not involved any of them in their plot to kidnap Loge. "Says we are to take our concern elsewhere. Says he wants no part of The Sinner's Palace or the Sutton family."

"He still ain't telling us what he's truly about with Tierney," Rafe added grimly. "But after that bastard dared to take the two of you as his prisoner, we had no choice but to accept the exchange."

"Damn it," Wolf cursed.

"We failed," Hart added. "Tierney is a cunning arsehole. He sent his men out the front of the shop to cause a distraction, and he approached us from the rear. We didn't see or hear him until his pistols were in our backs."

Grim disappointment twisted in Wolf's gut. They were no closer to answers than they had been before. Logan was still lost to them.

"Tierney is far more than a cunning arsehole," Jasper told them all, stroking his jaw with a thoughtful air. "My men have told me what's being printed at Tierney's place, and it ain't ordinary literature. It's Hampden Club pamphlets."

Hampden Clubs had been springing up over the last few years of discontent, meeting in secret, propagating reform literature. It was a dangerous business, and deuced easy to land on the wrong side of the Crown.

"A reformist?" Wolf asked, shocked at the prospect.

Loge had never been one to speak much about parliamentary matters or to have grievances against the government the way some did. That he would take up with a man determined to overthrow the government seemed damned unlikely.

"Not quite," Jasper said slowly. "I suspect it's something far less obvious."

"We believe our brother is a spy," Rafe elaborated. "Along with Tierney. One of Jasper's men followed Tierney to Whitehall. Tierney was disguised."

Whitehall was where the Home Office was kept. And with the Spa Fields riot having recently occurred, which had involved a gang of reformers who planned to attack the Tower of London, the Home Office and Bow Street were collectively on edge. Everyone was suspect.

"What of the moneylending and the print shop?" Hart asked. "You think it all a ruse?"

"Aye," Jasper said simply. "And a damned clever one at that."

"A dangerous one too," Wolf added. "If they are openly posing as Hampden men, that means Tierney and Loge are infiltrating the inner circles, and if these coves are as bloodthirsty as everyone supposes, if anyone discovers what they're about…"

He allowed his words to trail off, not wanting to give voice to his fears.

They had just finally found Loge, and he could not bear to

think of losing him. It was a bit more difficult to care as much about Tierney after the bastard had threatened himself and Hart with a pistol, and suggested Portia had deserved the violence she had suffered, even knowing he was Portia's half brother. But if what Jasper and Rafe suggested were true, it certainly made Loge's distancing himself and change of name clearer. Same for Tierney.

"It ain't going to be pretty," Jasper finished for Wolf.

"Speaking of pretty," Rafe drawled wryly, "Wolf, there's a lady awaiting you in your rooms. She didn't give a name, but she was rather desperate to see your ugly dial plate. We reckoned it was best to send her there while we waited for you to return."

In an instant, his exhaustion faded away.

Portia? Here?

It seemed impossible, and yet there was no other woman in his acquaintance who would seek him out in such a private way. And if Tierney had gone to her when he had disappeared, Wolf knew the reason why she had come. He had to see her.

Right. Bloody. *Now.*

He nodded. "I'd best see to her, then."

Jasper waved him away. "Go to your woman. There ain't any problem we're going to solve tonight. Tomorrow's another bloody day."

Jasper was right. If Loge was involved in something as treacherous as they supposed, there would be no solving it tonight. Without lingering another moment, Wolf left his brothers behind, all but racing from the office. He passed down the private hall in a blur and took the steps to his private chamber in threes.

Without bothering to knock, he burst through the door, his breath as ragged and weary as his heart. The room was illuminated by a brace of candles, and Portia's back was to him as she stood by the lone window. At his abrupt entrance, she spun about.

And Wolf's weariness was dashed when she came running toward him.

He caught Portia in his arms instinctively, holding her securely, as her sweet floral scent wrapped around him. He buried his face in her hair, though it was mostly bound in some manner of complicated knot that denied him the pleasure of the silken strands unruly and free.

"Countess, what are you doing here?" he asked.

She held him tightly in return, as if she feared he would disappear if she did not cling with all her might. "I need you."

Worry instantly surged, a knot tightening in his gut. "Is something amiss?"

"Yes," she said breathlessly.

He told himself he needed to remain calm. He could not spy any hint of an injury upon her in the low light. But if whomever had dared raise a hand to her had done so again, he could not be held accountable for his actions.

He ground his molars, forcing himself to attempt calm. "Tell me, love."

She tipped her head back, searching his gaze, her eyes wide and so astoundingly emerald. "Avery paid me a call. Archer, I suppose I should say. My brother is calling himself *Archer* Tierney now."

So Tierney *had* gone to her. Which meant he had not been nearly as indifferent to her plight as he had pretended earlier with his callous response to Wolf's telling him Portia had been struck by someone. And if he had reached her in such haste, it also meant Tierney had been watching Portia from afar, and possibly for years. He had known where to find her, despite the intervening time and change of circumstances.

"It is my bloody fault," Wolf muttered, his hold on her

tightening. "Is he the reason you're upset, love? What did the devil do?"

Her lower lip trembled and the undeniable sheen of tears glistened in her eyes. "He demanded to know who had done me violence. What happened? What did you tell him?"

It would seem Tierney was not entirely heartless. He obviously gave a damn about his sister and what happened to her. His reaction earlier had been feigned. Wolf could not entirely loathe him, knowing that. Even if the merry-begotten arsehole had seen him tied to a chair for the better part of an hour.

"It is a long story, what happened between myself and Tierney today," he managed, his voice thick with emotion. "I hope you are not angry with me for what I revealed to him. I only did so because I needed to know for certain if he was your half brother, for your sake."

"He is furious. I fear what he shall do."

"To you?" he asked, struggling to understand. "I'll not allow him to hurt you."

"No," Portia said softly, her gaze dipping to somewhere in the vicinity of the knot on his cravat. "Not to me. I do not believe he would ever harm me. He has always protected me. Whilst he could, of course. It has been many years since he last tried. But I am worried that what he aims to do will only make my circumstances worse, and I cannot bear it. I can bear anything, but I cannot lose my son."

She was trembling in his arms, the ferocity of her emotions eliciting an answering prick of tears to his own eyes. But that couldn't be right, could it? Wolf Sutton did not bloody *weep*.

He kissed her cheek, then brushed a stray tendril of chestnut hair from her face. "Why should you lose your son? I don't understand, love. Will you explain?"

"My brother," she said, a hitch in her voice.

"Tierney, aye. What are his threats?" he asked tightly, fury rising, replacing the sadness.

"Not him." Portia inhaled on a shaky breath, then exhaled slowly before continuing. "I have another brother, a legitimate one. He is now the Marquess of Granville. He is also the guardian of my son. Blakewell named my brother as Edwin's guardian in his will. As such, Granville takes precedence over me in every matter, from my son's education, to my own actions. He has warned me that if I displease him in any manner, he will take Edwin from me."

The naked fear in her eyes was akin to a fist in his gut. For a moment, Wolf could not breathe. Then, slowly, his protective nature roared to life.

"He is the one who struck you," he guessed. "The Marquess of Granville."

He was not asking. From the start, he had suspected a male relative. And he knew Portia well enough to understand she was a loving mother who would do anything in her power to protect her son and keep him at her side. If that meant bearing the violence of a heartless scoundrel who possessed untold power over her, she would do it.

Suddenly, her reticence in confiding in him made perfect, ugly sense. His chest went tight, the breaths he drew increasingly difficult. He ached for her. For her son. For what she had endured. How hopeless and helpless her life must be, living beneath the rule of her cruel brother.

"He was quite furious with me after he discovered I had come here to The Sinner's Palace at the urging of Mrs. Courteney. I was meant to have attended a social engagement he and his wife were hosting, but after…" Her words trailed off as she flushed, and he knew the reason.

He would never forget the day they had met, not as long as he lived and breathed. It was a part of his very soul now.

"I could not bring myself to go," she continued. "Not after what happened between us."

He knew what she meant, for it had shaken him to his core as well. He had already begun to fall in love with her then, he realized as he looked back. How swiftly it had happened. But he could not fathom his life without her in it.

"That night changed me," he told her.

*In more ways than I can say.*

"It changed me as well," she said softly.

*Say it now.*

*Tell her you've fallen in love with her.*

But nay, it was too soon. The moment was not right. The specter of her evil brother loomed, and for the first time, he truly understood.

"Your brother the marquess," he said slowly, hating to broach the subject, but needing to know. "You fear him."

Her gaze slid from his. "I fear the power he has over me."

"He has struck you before, has he not?" he guessed.

A shudder went through her frame, and he absorbed it as his hands glided over the small of her back in soothing strokes. It required all the restraint he possessed to keep from showing the anger roiling within him.

"Yes," she admitted.

Wolf had never felt a stronger urge to destroy another. And he'd been in bloody, knuckle-to-knuckle, knife-to-knife fights more times than he cared to count. The rookeries turned men against each other; it was simply the way of it. In his world, it was defend one's territory and family to the death if need be. But he had not known this visceral, raw desire to protect and defend the way he did for Portia and her son. It went to his marrow.

Still, he knew he could not show her the full extent of his rage. The fury within him was for one person only, and that was the Marquess of Granville. Wolf had no wish to further add to her upset. She seemed frightfully vulnerable in his arms, her tall frame pressed to his as if seeking succor.

He counted to five in his mind, formulating his response with care, before speaking again. "I am going to make certain he never 'arms you again."

*Christ*, he was slipping into the cant accent of his youth, the one he'd tried his damnedest to banish from his tongue with the guidance of the tutors Jasper had hired. But that was how strongly Wolf felt about this.

About *her*.

He understood, with blinding clarity, that he had never loved Lydia, not truly. Had never felt even a hint of an inkling of a goddamn crumb of what he felt for Portia.

"There is nothing you can do, Wolf," she said sadly. "I must answer to my brother."

It was not fair.

He wanted to rage and rail. To do something—anything. Even if it meant sacrificing himself.

"You should not be forced to answer to that swine. He is a cowardly villain," he bit out. "I do not understand why your husband would name him as the guardian of your son."

The color fled Portia's lovely face. And once again, her gaze darted away from his. "Blakewell had good intentions. He made the provisions he did because he did not trust me… because of my past, and because of my son."

Wolf frowned, struggling to understand her words. "Why would he not trust you? You are the best bloody mort I've ever known."

Her gaze flitted back to his, clinging, and she nibbled on her luscious lower lip. "My past." She paused, taking a deep breath before continuing. "Blakewell was not Edwin's father. I was wild and reckless in my first Season, which is how I became known as Lady Scandal. And I wrongly believed myself in love with a man who proved to be a villain. That man is Edwin's father, not Blakewell. The earl was unable to produce an heir, and he married me, knowing I was carrying another man's child, because he was ill and he wished for an heir. So you see? Given my past, Blakewell feared I would not be an improving influence upon my son."

She lowered her head at the last, as if she were too ashamed to meet his gaze.

*Bloody hell.*

"I don't see," Wolf bit out. "Not at all. Blakewell believed putting you at the mercy of a brute who would harm you was the best way to protect your son?"

Portia worried her lip some more. "I do not think he knew my brother would treat me as he has. Or perhaps he did, and he was acting in what he felt was the best interest of my son. He considered Edwin his heir and never treated him as if he were anything less than his true son. To the outside world, Edwin is his heir."

Wolf shook his head, angry at the earl for having left her at the mercy of such a scoundrel, angry at her for thinking her past should define her future. "We are not so very different, you and I. You believed yourself in love with a cove who didn't deserve you. I thought myself in love with a mort who didn't deserve me either. Hearts can be led astray. We should not have to pay the price for our mistakes forever."

"What I did was wrong. If anyone had discovered, I would have been forever ruined," Portia said. "Fortunately, only my family learned of my ignominy."

"And promptly married you off to an arsehole who forced you to live beneath your despicable brother's rule," he ground out. "I fail to see the fortune in that, Countess. You cared for someone. You believed him a good man. There's no wrong in thinking the best of someone."

Her emerald gaze searched his, her countenance troubled. "Most people would count me privileged to continue as I have, becoming a countess and maintaining my place in society rather than losing everything as so many others in my position have done."

How he hated her calm acceptance, the way she spoke of her circumstances as if she ought to be thankful for being beholden to a bastard of a brother who beat her when she displeased him. Was that the way of it for nobs? He supposed it was. Maintain a façade to please society. Follow the rules or perish. Never dare to have a heart. Never take a chance. Above all, never make a mistake.

And damn the Marquess of Granville to the fires of Hades for treating his own sister thus. The man clearly needed to reach an understanding. In the most difficult and painful manner possible. And Wolf was going to make that happen. He vowed it.

"Listen to me, love," he said, attempting to gentle his tone, for the force of his emotions at the moment was enough to down a grove of bloody trees. "It ain't a privilege to be forced to bend to the whims of a tyrant. It ain't a privilege for a man to raise his hand to you because you've gone against his dictates."

"That is the way of my world." Her tone was sad. Accepting. "I have not made the rules. I am merely forced to live within them. For my son's sake, I must."

"It is for your son's sake and yours both that you must *not*," Wolf countered grimly. "This ain't right. Your brother can raise his hand against the lad just as easily as he's done to you. And what will happen the next time you displease the marquess? I'm not going to wait to find out, Countess. We are going to fight. Together."

She was quick to shake her head. "No, you must not involve yourself. It would only go poorly, and I would never ask it of you."

Wolf's jaw clenched so hard it ached. He wanted—*needed*

—to help her. Doing so was more important than air. Because before she had miraculously appeared in his life, he had not known what it felt like to love someone. He'd thought he had, and he'd been wrong. This soul-deep, gut-clenching force, this need to protect, it was stronger than anything he had ever known. It was bigger than he was. And he would do anything, give every damned last part of himself, to keep her and her son safe.

"I know you wouldn't, but neither could I live with myself if I did nothing," he growled. "But it ain't right, what is happening to you. What you've been enduring."

"I have been enduring it for years," she said mildly. "You need not fret over me."

"The hell I needn't," he ground out. "I wasn't there before. I didn't know what was happening to you. But now I do, and I'll not stand for it. The woman I love is not going to be at the mercy of a cowardly, heartless scoundrel who thinks he ought to impose his will on his sister by beating her, for Christ's sake."

His entire body was shaking beneath the strain of his pent-up emotion. His hands were trembling. The effort of his words almost seemed more than he could bear. If he possessed a contrivance that could take him back in time, he would travel to the moment before that bastard had struck her. He would plant himself between them and dare the Marquess of Granville to raise his hand to an opponent matched to his strength. And then he would give him the basting he was owed.

"Say it again," Portia said, interrupting his tumultuous thoughts.

He blinked, struggling to understand her request. "Pardon?"

"*The woman I love*," she repeated softly, her vividly green eyes glistening. "That is what you said, is it not?"

Well, hell. So he had.

No point in denying it now. "Aye. I love you, Portia. My heart is yours. And I'll do everything in my power to keep you safe."

Whatever that meant, however it could be achieved. He understood the disparity in their stations. Whilst his siblings had married above themselves, he had no expectations of her. She was a countess, and her son was an earl. Her situation, thanks to her brother's guardianship of the lad, was untenable. Wolf would make no demands of her. All he wanted to do was love her.

Even from afar, though it would bloody well kill him.

She raised a hand to his cheek, her ungloved skin delicate and soft. The floral essence of her faintly teased his senses as she did so. *My God*, that touch. If he could have only one to last him for the rest of his life, it would be this. It would be hers. It would be the way she held his face as if he were not just beloved, but essential. As if he were fashioned of glass instead of a rough-hewn beast of the rookeries.

"I love you too, Wolf," she said.

And he could have died a happy man just then.

## CHAPTER 14

Portia had been dreadfully young and naïve the last time she'd said those three words to a man. That man—Edwin's father—had not been worthy of the sentiment. That man could not hold a candle to Wolf Sutton. Nor could any other.

Telling Wolf how she felt now was a risk.

But also a relief.

The moment the words left her, his expression turned so tender, an ache began deep inside her. Not desire, this time, although that was omnipresent in Wolf's company. But something far stronger. And the tears in her eyes at his protectiveness toward her and her son would no longer be restrained. They slipped free, sliding in hot trails down her cheeks.

"Christ, Countess. I can't abide it when you weep," he said gruffly, and then he kissed up each tear, catching them with his lips as he kissed her face with excruciating gentleness.

She clung to his broad shoulders, pressed her body more firmly to his. She wanted to be one with him. To pretend, at least for a few stolen moments, that she would never have to leave his side.

"Make love to me," she said, half command, half plea.

She did not have to make the request twice. Wolf took her in his arms, scooping her up and cradling her against his chest, despite their near parity in height. No one had ever picked her up thus, handling her with such ease. Not since she had been a child.

She held him tightly. "Wolf," she exclaimed, breathless. "I am too heavy for you!"

"You are perfect for me," he countered, stalking to his bed on the far end of the chamber.

She felt perfect in his arms, in his eyes.

She felt wild and exuberant, her heart beating far too fast, as if she had run a great distance. There were a hundred butterflies' wings moving furiously within her, emotion clamoring to be freed. She settled for kissing him. It was rash and impulsive, but perhaps no more so than running to him here at his gaming hell despite the risk. No more so than confessing her love for him and asking him to take her to bed.

It was all a risk.

But her heart would not be denied.

His lips were hot and firm beneath hers, and he kissed her as if he wished to consume her. A long, drugging kiss as he moved them across the room. So deep and powerful that she was surprised when they reached the bed and he dipped to settle her upon it. The world swirled and swayed around her. She had felt this way before, when she had consumed too much wine. She was drunk on Wolf, on love. Her head was too light for her body. And her emotions were too complex, too wild, to be contained within her.

"I am not perfect," she denied, thinking back to what he had said. "I have made so many mistakes in my life."

"Every mistake led you to me." He shucked his coat, dropping it to the floor, before his fingers moved to the buttons on his waistcoat. "And I'm damned glad you're here, Countess. Damned glad you're mine."

But she wasn't free to be his. Not truly. She would not think about that now. Could not bear to.

His waistcoat fell to the floor, and then he was yanking at his cravat, tossing that away too. She cared less about the state of her own garments than his. There was nothing she wanted more than to watch him. To see that big, beautiful body revealed to her once again.

Three buttons on his shirt sprang free, and then he caught a handful in his fist and hauled it over his head in one swift motion. There was his chest, wide and muscled and strong, embellished by the dragon in flight. Her position on the high bed meant that she was perfectly aligned to lean forward and press a kiss to his bare skin on one of the unfurled wings.

His skin was hot and smooth, his chest hairs tickling her lips as she kissed a trail along the dragon's tail, following it to his nipple. Her curiosity won, and she decided to see if he was as sensitive there as she was. Tentatively, she braced her hands on him, loving the feel of his flesh beneath her touch, and flicked her tongue over his nipple.

He made a low sound of pleasure, and then his fingers caught in her skirts, raising her gown and her petticoats simultaneously as he bunched it up to her thighs. The trace of his callused hands over her sensitive skin had her quivering. She felt bold and powerful here with him. As if anything were possible.

What a fanciful lie.

And yet, she would not dash it away.

Instead, she would revel in it while she could.

She kissed every bare swath of skin her lips could find,

inhaling deeply of his musky, masculine scent, so familiar and beloved, his warmth and vitality filling her with a renewed sense of hope. He was so firm, so strong. And he was hers. It was wrong of her, being here with him, but nothing and no one had ever felt more right.

Feeling bold, she kissed a path to his other nipple, this time nipping him lightly with her teeth. She loved the inking on his chest. Loved his body, his strength flexing beneath her traveling hands. Loved every part of her rugged, brutally handsome East End lover.

"Are you trying to bring me to my knees, Countess?" he asked, his voice deep and soft as velvet.

She smiled against his skin. "I can think of excellent uses for you in such a position, Mr. Sutton."

"Ah, damn it. You make it impossible to resist you." His fingers caught in her hair, gently tugging her head back so that her gaze met his hot, hazel stare. "I am not going to give you up, Portia. Not after tonight. You know that, don't you?"

There was no other way to answer him save one. All the hopelessness, the despair that held her captive when she thought about the impossibility of her circumstances, fell away beneath the healing, potent heat of that gaze. When he looked at her this way, she felt omnipotent. Believed that somehow, together, they could find a way.

"I know, my love," she told him, newfound strength lending her voice a conviction that had been absent until he had told her he loved her. "I don't want to live without you."

How freeing it felt to acknowledge that. To say the words aloud. Her fragile heart dared to hope it could be true.

"You don't have to," he vowed. "Not if I have anything to say about it."

"I need you." She allowed her hand to travel down his taut abdomen, over the tense muscle, the hot skin, until she moved over his trousers, where his cock was thick and hard.

She caressed the rigid length, wringing a moan from him as an answering ache began deep in her cunny, where she longed for him most. Between her thighs, she was wet and ready. Disrobing herself would take too much time. She was frantic for him.

*Now.*

He surged against her, and lowered his head until their mouths were sealed. This kiss was gentler than the last, but every bit as potent. He kissed her long and slow, his tongue dipping into her mouth to slide sinuously against hers. All the while, his fingers remained tangled in her hair, holding her still, angling her head so he could deepen the kiss. She was aflame, breasts heavy and full, nipples hard.

His other hand swept up her inner thigh, higher and higher until his fingertips met with her hungry flesh. And then, he did the most wicked thing. He cupped her, his touch possessive and firm, holding her cunny in his big, work-roughened hand. She liked the way it felt, the way he held her there, as if claiming the most elemental part of her. Acknowledging she was his in a pure, primitive form.

Oh, how she liked it.

And how she wanted more.

He withdrew from the kiss, still cupping her mound, and looked down at her, his countenance so intense, it stole her breath. "You're mine."

She did not even bother to deny it.

Wanton that she was, Portia parted her legs, arching into him. "Yes."

His clever fingers parted her folds, slicking the evidence of her desire up and down her seam. "So wet for me."

She would have answered him, but he circled over her entrance and sank a finger deep inside her then. All she could manage was a groan as her inner muscles clenched on him in glorious welcome that shot pleasure straight through her. The sensation was followed by the frantic need to release his cock from his trousers. She went to work on the fastenings, gratified when he sprang free, hot and hard in her waiting palm. He sank a second finger inside her, his thumb finding her swollen bud and stoking the fires of need ever higher. Each glance of his touch, coupled with the thrust of his fingers as he fucked her fast and furious, took her closer to the edge.

Her gaze was riveted to the sight of him, so thick and long, the bulbous tip ruddy and weeping. Had she been able to contort her body, she would have bent and taken him in her mouth, licked up his mettle, tasted him on her tongue. But his fingers were moving, angling, finding the center of all her pleasure, pinning her to the bed. Instead, she rubbed her thumb gently over his cock head, smoothing the pearlescent liquid over him. He was so wondrous, so large, overwhelmingly masculine. Everything she wanted.

"Look at me, Countess," he commanded.

And she did as he asked, helpless to do anything else, her stare moving from his demanding cock, following the trail of dark hair above it, over the twin juts of his hip bones, the cords of his belly, past his formidable chest graced with the dragon and its curling tail. All the way to his hazel eyes.

He continued his ministrations, crooking his fingers, gliding in and out of her wetness. It was so good, she cried out, rocking her hips as she chased the pleasure he gave, seeking more. So good, her eyelids fluttered closed as she surrendered.

"No," he rasped. "Don't close them. Don't shut me out. I want to watch you as I make you come."

She forced her eyes open. Forced herself to hold his gaze, to keep stroking him as he fucked her. It was unbearably erotic, his gaze holding hers, his fingers inside her, the silken heat of him in her hand. He increased the pressure and pace, and she lost control.

Pleasure burst open like a blossom.

She rode his hand, crying out as bliss rolled through her. Cried out and held his gaze, and it was so intimate, holding his stare, his fingers deep. So good, so perfect. When the last wave of pleasure subsided, he withdrew and brushed her fingers aside, gripping himself and guiding his cock to her entrance.

"I wanted you naked, but I can't wait another moment to be inside you where I belong," he said.

In the next breath, he thrust, and she was filled. So gloriously, deliciously full, the sensitivity brought on by her pinnacle heightening every sensation as his thick cock moved in and out of her. She did not care that she was still fully clothed. The need to be one with him supplanted all else.

Portia wrapped her legs around his waist, holding tight to his shoulders as he pumped his hips, driving deep and then retreating before slamming into her again, finding that same place that caused her to go wild. She was even wetter than before, the slickness of her cunny making a sound that echoed in the small room, along with their panting breaths.

"Kiss me," she said breathlessly. "I want your mouth on mine."

With a growl, he did as she asked, sealing their lips together, taking her mouth in a kiss that was voracious. They tongues met. Teeth nipped. And she was falling apart again. He made another low sound that told her he was fast losing control as well, and the knowledge had her spending once more. Her orgasm was wilder than the last. She clenched on his cock, and he drove into her as pleasure tore through her. But this time, he did not withdraw.

Instead, the warmth of his seed filled her.

She kissed him fiercely, showing him with her lips and tongue the depth of her emotion as she held tight to him, draining him of every last drop. She wanted it all. Wanted every part of him. Wanted him.

*Forever.*

The realization hit her, along with a returning sense of awareness.

They had taken a risk. And it was a risk she had taken before. But this was different. *Wolf* was different. She did not feel a modicum of regret.

He broke the kiss, pressing his lips reverently to her throat as he buried his face there, his breathing harsh, his body still joined with hers. "Let me take care of you, Portia. Let me love you. If you'll not marry me, I understand. I'm not a nob, and I'll never be one. But I *am* the man who loves you, and I want to make you my wife."

It seemed impossible.

Granville would never allow her to marry a man like him without exacting some manner of revenge. But here in Wolf's arms, his body still pulsing inside her, anything felt possible. Maybe she had not learned a single lesson in all her years. Perhaps she was the same foolish girl she had once been. Whatever the reason, she rubbed her cheek against Wolf's, kissed his ear, his hair, any part of him she could reach.

"Yes," she said. "I cannot live like this, without you, any longer."

It was the truth. She wanted this man. Wanted his love. Wanted to be free. Needed him, if she were honest.

And she had to believe it was possible.

Somehow.

If she did not have hope, what else was left?

"Trust me, love," Wolf said softly, as if sensing the direction of her troubled musings. "I'll find a way."

~

Wolf held Portia on his lap as the carriage rocked over familiar, rutted roads, taking them from the East End back to where she truly belonged.

To Mayfair.

To her town house and her butler and her gilt-edged world.

Unlike the other occasions when they had parted, however, he had hope. And determination. Because she loved him. He loved her. And he was going to make her his wife. He would not stop until he did.

"Damn it," he said on a heavy sigh, tightening his arms around her, for he knew they were nearing Blakewell House and she would have to depart. "I never want to let you go."

She nuzzled his throat, those silken lips of hers teasing skin he had not even realized was sensitive before. "Did you mean what you said back at The Sinner's Palace?"

"That I love you?" He kissed her crown, thankful she had removed her hat and veil for the carriage ride, so that he was not deprived the luxury of her smooth, chestnut hair beneath his lips. "Of course I meant it. How could you doubt?"

"Not that." Her fingers swept into the hair at his nape, sending a pleasant thrill down his spine. "I know you love me, Wolf. I feel it when we are together, and even when we are not. You have shown me in everything you do."

He kissed her again, smiling against her part. "Christ. At least I'm not an utter failure, then."

She chuckled softly, and this sound, too, was pleasing to his senses. She did not laugh nearly enough. *Bloody hell*, had he ever heard her levity? He did not think so.

"You could never be a failure. What I meant was...when you said you wanted to marry me. Do you, truly?" she asked, her voice hesitant.

"I have never wanted anything more," he admitted, his voice hoarse with suppressed emotion. "As long as you will have me, that is. If you do not wish it, I understand. I'm not a lord. I'm not elegant or polished, and I don't know a goddamned thing about proper manners. Hell, I can't even make a proposal without cursing…"

She pressed a finger to his lips, staying further speech. "Hush. It would be my honor to be your wife. I did not have a choice the first time I married. This next time—the last time —I want my husband to be the man who loves me. The man who *truly* loves me."

Aye, that was him. He had teased his brothers mercilessly about falling in love with their women. And now, look at him. Utterly besotted, his countess on his lap where he wanted to forever keep her.

Actually, he would prefer to keep her forever in his bed, but that was another matter, and if he thought upon it for too long, he was likely to get a raging cockstand…

*Too late.*

She shifted on his lap, the friction of her shapely bottom against his rapidly stiffening prick enough to make him groan.

Portia tilted her head back, studying him through the low light reflecting from the carriage lamps. She was cloaked in shadows, but despite the darkness, she was the loveliest sight he had ever beheld.

"It would be my honor to be your husband," he said. "And I also meant it when I told you we will come to an understanding with your devil of a brother. Do you suppose your lad will accept a rough, rookeries-born beast married to his beautiful mama?"

He had only met the boy on one occasion. His impression of the young lord was that he was intelligent and kind like his mother, and headstrong too. Wolf adored his twin nieces. He thought Elizabeth and Anne would get on well with the lad, as they were nearly of an age. And Wolf would be more than pleased to be a father figure to the boy.

"Edwin will love you as I do," Portia reassured him. "I have no doubt of that."

Still, Wolf was going to have to spend some time with the lad. He owed it to Portia and her son to do this right. Not to make a muck of things. They deserved happiness and security.

Which reminded him.

"I am coming to you tomorrow," he told her. "Be prepared. I intend to interview your domestics. We will discover which of them is running back to your brother with a wagging tongue. You ought to be able to trust those beneath your own damned roof. They are in your employ, not his."

"I was too fearful to attempt it myself," she said quietly.

And that killed him.

Her brother was a bloody monster.

A monster Wolf was going to stop.

"You needn't fear any longer, my love." He kissed her crown once more as the carriage rocked to a halt in the mews behind her town house.

And he knew just the man to help him accomplish it.

~

IT HADN'T TAKEN Jasper's men long to discover where Archer Tierney laid his head at night. The address, however, was something of a surprise. An elegant town house tucked away on a street not far from Grosvenor Square. Aye, it was an esteemed address for an East End moneylender-turned-printer, that much was bloody certain. Recently leased. Apparently, Mr. Tierney was moving up in the world even further.

The reason for Tierney's change of address was not Wolf's concern, however.

His role as Portia's half brother was.

And so it was that after leaving Portia safely at Blakewell House, Wolf found himself rapping on the door of the stately home Tierney was currently calling his.

The hour was late.

The butler who answered was understandably miffed, not just by the call, but by the appearance of a lowborn ruffian at the door. Wolf knew he didn't look the part of a gentleman. And he wasn't one, so that was just fine by him. He preferred black, his cravats were simply knotted, and he didn't give a damn about walking sticks and top hats and pocket watches, nor any of the other trappings of nobs. Simplicity was what he liked, and he wouldn't apologize for it. Besides, a man could be a marquess and dress in the finest togs, but it didn't make his insides any less despicable. Portia's brother, Lord Granville, was proof of that.

"Mr. Wolf Sutton to see Tierney," he said to the butler without hesitation.

"The master ain't at 'ome," the cove declared, shocking Wolf with his accent. For despite resembling an elegant butler, the man didn't possess the bland tones of one who had been raised to service in a fancy lord's estate. Rather, his speech bore the mark of the rookeries.

Same as Wolf's.

*Interesting.*

But never mind that. He was attempting to keep Wolf from his objective, and that would not bloody well hold.

It was a predictable denial the butler had issued. Tierney

would not wish to entertain callers here at such an hour. Perhaps not ever. It was a curious thing, this house, much like the man himself. A conundrum wrapped in a mystery. Why would a man who was printing revolutionary pamphlets live in such a grand abode, even if the printer's shop and the house were both newly acquired? It made no sense.

But the specifics of Tierney's circumstances were a question for another day. Wolf had something far more important to attend to.

*Portia.*

*My woman.*

"I'll not leave until he sees me," Wolf countered, putting his booted foot on the threshold, lest the man attempt to snap the door closed in his face. "You'd best tell him it concerns his sister."

The butler pinned him with a rather ferocious glare. "Wait where ye are, or it ain't going to go well for you."

The threat did not concern him.

The moment the servant turned and disappeared into the house, Wolf pressed his advantage, slipping into the entry through the door which had been left slightly ajar. He closed it at his back, for whilst this was the West End, there was no telling what manner of miscreants were afoot at night. Himself included.

*Eh,* while he was at it, why wait as he'd been instructed? He wanted this matter to be settled tonight. Which meant Tierney was going to have to be flushed up, like a startled bird, one way or another.

Wolf followed the sound of the butler's footsteps, which led him down a carpeted hall and to a door, where the butler stopped and rapped. Fortunately, his youthful habit of housebreaking had imbued Wolf with stealth. Despite his large size, he could travel silently, undetected, with ease. The butler did not even know he had been followed until it was too late.

"There's a cove at the door who says 'e wishes to see ye, sir," the butler was saying. "Claims it's about yer sister—stop there, ye bleedin' arsehole. I told ye to wait at the damned door. Say the word, sir, and I'll gut 'im like a fish."

The man—not any manner of true butler—sputtered as Wolf slipped past him, unconcerned. The room he entered was clearly being used as an office of sorts. He had the vague impression of intricate, dark woodwork and pictures dotting the walls, before he spied Tierney seated at a desk, a fire in the grate behind him and a glowing cigar in his mouth.

Tierney shot to his feet at Wolf's appearance, plucking the cigar from his lips. "Sutton. What the hell are you doing here?"

"Ought I to call for anyone, sir?" the henchman asked behind Wolf, sounding agitated.

"I need to have a patter with you," Wolf addressed Tierney, ignoring the other man. "It's about your sister and your brother."

Tierney blew a ring of smoke into the air, his expression remaining unconcerned, though his jaw clenched, the only sign of his displeasure. "Carry on then, Lucky. I'll see to Mr. Sutton."

"Be ye certain, sir?"

"Aye," Tierney drawled, raising a brow as he held Wolf's gaze. "Wouldn't harm a fly, this one. Besides, he's already well acquainted with my pistols, aren't you, Sutton?"

Wolf glared back at him. "I've seen your barking irons. Not afraid of them, neither."

Tierney grinned, then flicked his gaze to the other man in the room. "Thank you, Lucky. You may go."

The henchman glowered, clearly disapproving. "I'll be near if ye need me, sir."

Definitely not a butler, that one. Some manner of guard? Certainly, a criminal of some sort.

Wolf waited for the door to click closed before advancing on Tierney, crossing the carpets. "What do you know of the Marquess of Granville?" he demanded.

Tierney's lip curled. "I know I can't kill him, much as I'd like to."

Wolf stopped as he reached the desk, the scent of Tierney's cigar smoke swirling around him. "I understand you've been to see Portia."

"And I understand you've been bedding my sister, Sutton." Calmly, Tierney took a long, slow puff of his cigar. "I may not be able to kill Granville, but you…you're another matter, ain't you?"

"I'll thank you not to speak so crudely about her," Wolf ground out. Planting a facer on a cove had never been more tempting. "I'm in love with your sister, and I'm going to marry her. All I want to do is to protect her and her son."

"You love her," Tierney repeated, his expression as harsh as his voice.

It was plain to see he did not believe in the emotion, and he most certainly did not believe in Wolf either.

"As I said."

Tierney puffed on his cigar once more. "And how am I to trust this ain't about you and the rest of your brothers having your backs up over my business partner?"

It nettled, hearing the man refer to Logan as his business partner, particularly if Tierney and Loge were involved in something as dangerous as Jasper suspected. But as much as Wolf loved his brother, Loge was not the reason he had come here.

"Because this is about making certain the Marquess of Granville can't beat your sister ever again," Wolf said grimly. "You know him. I'd wager you understand what he's capable of. Portia told me you'd saved her from her brother's wrath in your youth, and that the two of you were close before you were taken away."

Tierney's nostrils flared. "I've been planning to destroy that bastard for years. This is a convenient opportunity to make use of the ammunition I've been collecting."

Ah, so Portia had not been wrong, then, when she had shared more with him in the aftermath of their lovemaking. Tierney *was* planning some means of revenge upon Granville. But Wolf was still not certain whether Tierney was trustworthy, or whether his plans would truly free Portia of that tyrant's rule.

"What ammunition do you have against him?" he asked. "Granville is her son's guardian, and it's left her in a terrible bind."

Tierney calmly exhaled another small cloud of smoke. "I've the best kind of ammunition there is against a coward like the marquess. All his vowels. Seems my dear brother may have been born on the right side of the blanket, but he doesn't know how to keep from bleeding his funds at every gaming table in London."

"Not every hell," Wolf remarked. "I don't recall him darkening the door of The Sinner's Palace, and I never forget a name or a face."

"Only the best for the marquess." Tierney raised a mocking brow. "No offense, Sutton, but your ramshackle affair ain't precisely up to the standards of some of the more exacting members of the *ton*. Higher-risk games to lose all their blunt in, etcetera."

So the Marquess of Granville, in addition to being a

sister-beating sack of shite, was also an inveterate gambler. And a poor one, if the man before Wolf was to be believed.

"What do you intend to do with the debts?" he asked.

Tierney grinned around his cigar before removing it and delivering another puff of smoke. "I'm going to call them in. I fancy the notion of having him beneath my thumb for the rest of his misbegotten life, I'll not lie."

"There's a possibility the debts won't prove sufficient," Wolf said, for now that he was privileged to the information that the marquess liked to lose his purse at the green baize, a plan was beginning to form. "I need to be certain he'll not interfere in my plans to marry your sister, and that he will not carry out his threat of taking her son from her."

And he'd thought long and hard about how he could obtain such reassurances of his own. He'd had a number of threats of his own that he could make, of course. But his, coupled with the debts Tierney held, and the new idea taking shape, ought to be enough.

"Why should I bring you into it?" Tierney demanded, scowling. "Don't need your help, Sutton, and I never did."

"Because I'm in love with Portia, and because I must be assured Granville can never hurt her again. I'll not marry her if there remains a possibility that bastard could take her son or cause her any other manner of mischief."

Tierney's gaze, the same vivid green as Portia's, narrowed. "You'll need to prove yourself if you mean to marry my sister, you know. Portia deserves to have a say in her future as much as anyone, and she certainly deserves better than what she's endured, married off to that old codger, Blakewell and then kept beneath Granville's thumb all these years. I'd have slipped poison into his wine by now if I were her."

"Poison in the wine ain't a bad notion," Wolf said. "None

more deserving than him. But we'll do it another way, one that leaves no doubt as to Portia's freedom."

"And how's that?" Tierney demanded.

A slow sense of peace slid over Wolf. "By inviting him to a game with a reward he can't resist. A game where he'll have the chance of a cat in hell without claws of emerging the victor."

## CHAPTER 15

*The* game was *vingt-et-un*.

The dealer was Wolf Sutton.

And those were two very bad facts for the Marquess of Granville, who, in the turn of a few cards, was going to lose his tremendous Derbyshire estate. And from the look of him —pale, fidgeting, his fingers tapping on the table in a rhythm of worry only he could hear—the marquess knew it as well.

What he did not know, and what he could not know, was that his very presence this evening was part of an elaborate spider's web which had been lovingly spun, all with the intention of catching his wretched arse within it.

In this instance, Wolf was the spider.

Granville was the fly.

And Wolf was about to attack.

Luring the Marquess of Granville to The Sinner's Palace II had been easier than Wolf had supposed. Fortunately, the new, fashionable gaming club in a part of London nobs deemed more acceptable to their lofty sensibilities was open. Also fortunately, many of Wolf's siblings had established connections in the *ton*. Viscount Lindsey, who had married

Wolf's sister Pen, had proven an immeasurable boon when he had offered his patronage. He had also been certain to laude the glories of the diversions being offered there quite vociferously in the presence of the marquess. The next day, an exclusive invitation had been delivered to Granville's town house.

But prior to that invitation's issuance, Archer Tierney had sought out his half brother for a meeting. As planned, he had informed Granville that he was in possession of his vowels and that he intended to call them in. For a princely sum, to be offered within one sennight, Tierney would surrender them.

Granville's desperation, coupled with Lindsey's approval of The Sinner's Palace II and the invitation to the game of chance, had led to the marquess accepting. The players had been chosen with care. The funds being wagered were immense. A few rounds having been played, the marquess was already heavily in debt. A debt he could not afford, given the massive sums he owed to Tierney.

But fortunately, in addition to being an expert house cracksman, Wolf was also damned adept at cheating at cards. His fingers were fast. No one had ever caught him in the act. Not even any of his brothers, and Jasper had trained them all to thoroughly watch each patron at the tables with a keen eye to making sure none were cheating. Aye, most of his talents were admittedly criminal in nature.

Still, he reasoned that if there were ever a time to engage in his illicit talents, it was now. Portia and her son needed him. And with the help of Tierney, Wolf was going to make damned sure they would have him.

Forever, just as he had promised her. After all, Wolf Sutton was a man of action. Just as he had proven to Portia the day she had first taken his gaming hell by storm. And then later, when she had taken his heart in just the same fashion.

Wolf had arranged the hands well. He had lost intentionally. Allowed some of the players to linger as the wagers grew. But now?

Now, he was going to win.

Wolf had one-and-twenty in the cards before him.

He met the marquess's gaze, which was the same green as Portia's and Tierney's. But flat and cold instead, the whites shot through with blood.

"Another card, my lord?" he asked Granville, knowing full well that the marquess had a hand that totaled twenty.

Granville glanced down at his cards again, clearly calculating the risk.

He had wagered his palatial home, his massive estate. The crown jewel of his unentailed property. All he had remaining.

The marquess shook his head, declining. Containing the surge of violent relief inside himself was almost too much to bear as Wolf maintained his composure and completed the round, flipping over his own cards to reveal the winning hand.

"Christ!" shouted Granville, pounding the table with his fist. "It cannot be. I had twenty! The odds of the dealer making *vingt-et-un* are nearly impossible."

With a deadly serious expression, Wolf held the stare of the fuming marquess. "Are you suggesting our establishment does not offer fair games, my lord?"

Granville's cheeks went ruddy as he no doubt realized the dangers inherent in such an implication. Men were called out, dueled, and died for lesser insults.

"No," the marquess muttered, shaking his head, before surging abruptly to his feet. "But this cannot be. It simply cannot be."

"I am afraid it *can* be, Lord Granville," he said calmly. "Indeed, it *is*. The Sinner's Palace is now in possession of your Derbyshire estate."

The marquess's hands opened and closed into fists at his sides. "No, no. I cannot have lost it."

Wolf clenched his jaw as he nodded to one of the lads to replace him at the table and slipped around the edge to pull abreast of the marquess. "You have, my lord. Just now."

Granville remained in denial, face red, fists balled tightly as if he intended to strike someone.

*Good,* thought Wolf. *Strike me. Take out your rage on someone your own size, you cowardly vermin.*

But the marquess did not. Shock seemed to have overtaken him. The Derbyshire estate was worth a veritable king's ransom, and Wolf knew it. He had counted upon it, in fact.

"Would you care to accompany me to a private room my lord?" he asked solicitously, hating that he was being forced to continue the charade of being polite for a few more moments. "In circumstances such as these, it's customary for privacy to be required. Indeed, perhaps there is an understanding that can be reached between yourself and The Sinner's Palace."

"I..." the man faltered, his gaze going wild as his panic continued to heighten.

Wolf had seen such a reaction before when patrons had wagered far more than they could afford at the tables. In the past, he had felt sympathy for the poor nobs.

But he didn't feel a hint of contrition for the Marquess of Granville. He was about to reap the mercy he had sown.

Which was to say not a goddamn bit.

"Come," Wolf ordered him, taking command of the situation and guiding Granville across the room to a discreet door.

He knocked twice, and it swung inward, opening to reveal one of the private dining rooms. Within, Jasper, Rafe, and Hart awaited, looking as menacing as they were capable of being.

"My lord," Jasper said coolly in greeting.

Granville hesitated, and Wolf crowded him from behind, leaving him no choice save crossing the threshold as Wolf stepped inside as well and closed and bolted the door at his back.

"What is the meaning of this?" Granville demanded.

"So good of you to ask," Wolf drawled. "You lost your Derbyshire estate this evening, my lord. And, unless I'm mistaken, you are also severely indebted to a moneylender by the name of Archer Tierney."

"A half brother of yours, so I'm told," Jasper added.

"A vast sum," Rafe said.

"The sort that's going to leave you bankrupted," Hart concluded.

"But seeing that we're good-natured coves," Wolf continued, "we are willing to make a concession."

Granville's nostrils flared. "I was tricked. The four of you are confederates of that swine Tierney. I should have known!"

"You were not tricked," Jasper snapped. "You are a terrible gambler. You need only to look at your vowels to realize that for yourself, Granville. The only person in this room who tricked you is yourself."

That was not entirely true, but again, Wolf felt nary a hint of compunction at the lie. Suttons were loyal to one another above all else, and Portia was about to become a Sutton. As his brothers had assured him, she was already family.

"We don't take kindly to the suggestion we ain't an honest establishment," Rafe added, cracking his knuckles.

"Not kindly at all," Hart said, his expression deadly.

"We are willing to offer an exchange, however," Wolf said. "The Derbyshire property will be restored to you when you surrender your role as legal guardian of your nephew. The new guardian, appointed by you, will be your sister."

"I need the property to pay my debts to that son-of-a-whore Tierney," Granville said. "But why the hell should you care who is the guardian of my nephew unless… My God, I never believed she would have sunken so low. That wanton, faithless, witless—"

"Enough," Wolf bit out, cutting off any further insults Granville would have paid Portia. "You will also never again raise a hand to her. You will never pay her another call. You will never burden her with your presence in her life. And if you do, well, we have men everywhere in our employ. No telling when one of them might steal into your rooms while you're asleep."

He was treading carefully. He had not directly threatened a peer of the realm, and nor had he raised a hand against the marquess. But he was not taking any chances, much as he wished to smash his fist into Granville's nose for the vile accusations he had made about Portia and for the harm he had done to her.

"But all that unpleasantness can be avoided with ease," Jasper continued smoothly. "As long as you do as we ask."

"What choice have I?" Granville muttered, looking impotent and furious. "I'll sign the whelp away, and my doxy of a sister, too."

Wolf's own fists clenched at his sides this time, but he held himself in check. For his future with Portia was far more important than the Marquess of Granville.

"See that you do," he ground out, the only reaction he would allow. "With all haste."

"Or we ain't going to be responsible for what befalls you," Hart added with an ominous air of warning.

PORTIA WAS in her salon with Edwin when Riggs announced their visitor.

"Mr. Wolf Sutton, my lady."

If the butler thought it odd that a gentleman was calling upon her at such an unfashionable hour of the evening, he gave no indication. And she was grateful for his steadfast loyalty. With Wolf's help, she had discovered the tutor Granville had hired for her son and one of her grooms had been working at the behest of her brother to spy upon her. Both the odious Mr. Leslie and the groom had been dismissed.

When her brother had discovered the news, he had been predictably furious, but Portia had instructed Riggs to deny the marquess entrance. She had no notion how long her reprieve would last, and she could only hope Wolf's plan meant she would never have to face Granville again on her own.

Thanks to Wolf, she trusted everyone in her household now.

And she was breathing a bit easier. However, her heart would not truly be free of the heavy weights resting upon it until Wolf told her how his plan to foil her brother had gone tonight.

"Please show him in, Riggs," she said, impressed with herself for maintaining her calm instead of catching her gown in both hands and racing to where Wolf undoubtedly awaited them in the front hall.

She was afraid to hope he had been successful. Afraid to believe she could finally be free of living beneath her brother's thumb. That she would never again need to fear losing her son. That she would never again be forced to endure a hand raised against her.

Riggs bowed and departed.

"Mama," Edwin said into the silence, his eyes still firmly fixed upon his drawing, which was, of course, another dragon.

His tongue was planted firmly in the corner of his mouth, an adorable habit of his that told her when he was concentrating. His pastel crayon swept over the page as he worked on the dragon's tail.

"Yes, darling?" she asked, moving to him and stroking his hair. It was growing rather long, she thought, and was soon in need of a trim. She leaned over him, examining his progress with his latest sketch. "This one is even more formidable than the last," she observed.

"How do you think Mr. Sutton will like it?" Edwin asked fretfully. "I do hope he will be impressed. He told me the last one was bang up."

*Bang up.*

She smiled. That sounded precisely like something Wolf would say. They had been meeting as often as possible over the past few days in clandestine locations, and he had encouraged her to bring Edwin along. They had rendezvoused at the park. A book shop. At his eldest brother's town house. At Hattie's. Everywhere they could find each other. Stolen moments. Wolf was always sweetly attentive to Edwin, and her son seemed to eat up the attention. It had not occurred to her just how starved he had been for a paternal figure until Wolf had begun a more consistent presence in her son's life. The two of them had become fast friends, much to her heart's relief.

"I am sure he will be impressed," she assured her son.

"Who will be impressed?" asked a familiar, deep voice.

Portia looked up to find the tall, imposing figure of the man she loved at the threshold. "Wolf," she said, searching his countenance for any indication that the evening's efforts had been a success.

"Mr. Sutton!" exclaimed Edwin, rising from the chair at her writing desk and racing across the room with a complete disregard for his composure.

She did not bother to correct him, for the world would take away her son's boyish exuberance and natural innocence soon enough. No need for her to admonish him. The unbridled joy he felt at seeing Wolf warmed her heart in a way nothing else could.

"If it isn't my favorite lad," Wolf said, bending down and opening his arms. Edwin rushed forward and into Wolf's embrace. "It is good to see you too, son."

*Son.*

The word made Portia's heart swell with renewed hope.

"How did it go?" she asked, unable to wait a moment more, her throat thick with emotion.

"Well," Wolf said, his hazel stare warm as it held hers. "It's done."

*Done.*

Another word that made her feel as if she were closer to being free. To being the woman she wanted to be. Not Lady Scandal. Not the Countess of Blakewell. But rather, Wolf Sutton's wife. Edwin's mother. *Herself*, full stop.

"You mean…" Her words faltered as she struggled to string them into a semblance of order, so strong was her reaction.

Also, she had done her utmost to keep the truth from Edwin. He was aware that his uncle was not a good man, but the rest could wait until he was old enough to understand. Wolf knew to be circumspect as well in the presence of her son.

"An understanding has been reached, and you needn't worry any longer," he said, elaborating just enough so that she would understand without a doubt that her brother had lost his Derbyshire estate at the tables, and that the Suttons were now holding it for ransom, in exchange for Edwin's guardianship. Wolf straightened, then gave Edwin's too-long hair an affectionate ruffle. "Your hair needs a trim, lad."

"I like it long," Edwin said shyly, touching the ends. "It looks like yours, sir."

"Here now, no more of that *sir* business," he told Edwin with a wink. "You must call me Wolf. And if it's long hair you prefer, then I'm not one to quarrel."

Portia could not tear her gaze away from him.

He was so handsome in his evening finery, dressed head to toe in black, save the crisp white of his shirt and cravat. But it was not just his arresting looks that held her in thrall. It was everything else about him too. His generosity of heart, his loyalty, his tenderness, his caring, his protective nature. Because of him, she had been able to find her brother again, and although she knew it would take some time to heal the old wounds between herself and Archer, she had every hope that she would one day have a relationship with her brother again. After all, Archer had been invaluable in their plot to save her from Granville. She was indebted to him as well.

"You look bang up to me," Edwin told Wolf, tearing her from her thoughts.

Portia smiled at his repeat of Wolf's phrase. His hero worship of Wolf filled her with the sort of contented happiness she had only dreamed could one day be hers.

"High praise, lad." Wolf executed a formal bow. "Thank you."

His antics made Edwin laugh, and Portia joined in.

"There," Wolf said, looking at her as if he had just beheld something miraculous. "I'd give my left arm for more of that."

"More of what?" she asked, chuckling some more at his hyperbole.

"Your laughter," he answered softly, tenderly. "Your smile."

"Mama has been smiling more than ever recently," Edwin confided, as if she were not standing there in the chamber with them, overhearing every word.

But then, she *had* been smiling more. And laughing, too. There was a reason for the lightness in her life, chasing the darkness that had clouded it for far too long.

"I hope to make your mother smile even more, lad," Wolf told Edwin. "But I've something to ask you first."

"Oh?" Edwin asked, puffing out his chest in a sudden show of grandiosity.

"Aye." Wolf sank to his haunches so that he was at the same level as her son, eying him solemnly, the levity of just a moment before fading. "I am wondering if it would be acceptable to you if I were to marry your mama."

"I think I would like that very much," Edwin replied solemnly. "But you had better ask Mama what she thinks of the notion."

Wolf's gaze flicked to hers. "Will you be my wife, Portia?"

"Yes," she said, the prick of happy tears rushing to her eyes. "Had you any doubt as to my answer?"

He grinned. "I reckoned I knew, but as the lad here pointed out, a gentleman always asks his lady for her permission."

Wolf's wife. How impossible it seemed! How wondrous.

"It would be my honor," she said softly, meaning those words.

"No, love. It would be mine." Wolf reached into his coat and withdrew a small case, extending it to Edwin. "I've a gift for you, lad, to celebrate the occasion."

"For me?" Edwin's eyes went wide as he accepted the case

and opened it to reveal a neat new set of pastel crayons. "Oh, sir! Thank you! Now I may have a set to keep in the library instead of needing to carry them about."

"Of course, lad." Wolf rose to his full height, his gaze returning to Portia as he withdrew yet another, smaller object from his coat. "And I've a gift for you as well."

A ring, she realized.

"A symbol of my affection for you," he said.

Portia moved toward him at last, joining him and Edwin and extending her hand that he might slide the ring on her finger. It was fashioned of gold filigree, adorned with an emerald.

"To match your eyes," he added. "I hope you like it, Countess."

"I love it," she said softly, admiring the ring as it slid perfectly upon her finger, guided by Wolf. "And I love you, Wolf Sutton."

"I love you, too," Wolf returned, reaching down to put an arm around Edwin's shoulders and draw him into their circle. "I love you both."

Portia held her son and her future husband into her embrace, her heart impossibly full.

# EPILOGUE

*W*olf's wife was trouble.
    The very best sort.
She was also on his lap, which was making it deuced difficult to concentrate on the ledgers which had been awaiting him on the desk. With all the changes in circumstance his siblings had gone through—marriages, babies, new business endeavors, the list was endless—they had taken to sharing the duties that corresponded with running two successful gaming clubs. And sharing meant whomever was about attended to anything that required addressing.

On this particular evening, it was the ledgers, which had been neglected for about a week now that Pen was nearly ready to have her babe. But some day soon, when Portia was at her lying in for the child growing now in her womb, someone else would be taking Wolf's place as he tended to his wife and their son. Aye—*son*. He could not contain the pride that rose within him at the thought, for young Edwin had asked several weeks before if he might call Wolf *Papa* now. And Wolf had never felt more complete.

"You have a penchant for disrupting me in this office," he

drawled, not regretting Portia's surprise appearance at The Sinner's Palace one whit.

The blasted tallies behind her could wait.

She smiled as she linked her arms around his neck, her vibrant eyes glittering into his. "It is the first place we met. Do you remember what you asked me that day?"

He thought for a moment. "All I recall about that day is what happened on this desk."

Hungry kisses, his fingers gliding over her silken quim. Aye, he remembered that.

"You asked me if I was lost," she said.

Ah, yes. So he had.

"You were wearing a ball gown and satin slippers," he pointed out wryly. "It ain't every day that a countess appears in The Sinner's Palace, dressed like a goddess and smelling like a garden in bloom."

She gave him a mock pout that made him long to kiss her senseless. "I hope it was just that one day, and that I was the only countess you ever seduced on this desk."

"It was, and you are." His head dipped, and he claimed those luscious lips for a moment before withdrawing to meet her gaze. "I reckon I'm about to seduce her on this bloody chair now as well."

She smiled again and he kissed the corner of her lips. "I'm not a countess any longer. I'm Mrs. Wolf Sutton now."

He grinned, pride and love crashing together in his heart and making it beat fast. "Damned right, you are."

"And it is she who is about to seduce you on this chair," she said wickedly as one of her hands slid down his chest in a tantalizing caress. "Not the other way around."

"I'm not about to stop her," he said.

"Good." She kissed his jaw, his ear, his throat.

"Christ," he growled when her tongue licked against his skin. "I'm harder than a fire iron."

Her fingers danced over the fall of his trousers. "And every bit as hot."

His head fell back against the chair and he arched into her knowing touch. "Perhaps you ought to open those buttons and feel for yourself just how much."

"Oh yes," she murmured. "I think I shall."

But rather than pluck a button from its moorings, she prolonged his torture, wriggling on his lap and tormenting his poor, aching cock with the tease of her full bottom moving over him.

"Damn it, love," he growled, clutching her waist as if that would stay her movement. "What are you trying to do, wife, kill me?"

"Not at all." His Siren slid to the carpets before him, on her knees. She glanced up at Wolf from beneath lowered lashes. "I only want to please you, husband."

She pleased him more than he could ever possibly convey with mere words. Even his actions, he feared, failed miserably at showing her just how loved she was. But he did his damnedest every day, to show her in every possible way.

Her nimble fingers worked the buttons on his trousers, unhooking one. He was pulsing, his cock weeping with the need to be in her hands, in her mouth. And she knew it, the sly minx. Knew just the effect she had on him. The other button slid free. The placket fell down, and cool air kissed his prick as it sprang forward, hard and ready for her.

*Blast.* They could be interrupted at any moment. He had to stop her.

Wolf glanced at the door, which was firmly closed, but not locked, and tried to summon his control. "Someone could come in, love. You had best not—"

His words died away into a groan at the velvet heat of her mouth engulfing him. She took him deep, all the way to the back of her throat, and held him there before slowly withdrawing, sucking his cock along the way.

"Portia," he said, half moan, half protest.

She gripped his shaft firmly and flicked her tongue around the head of his cock, before pressing her tongue into his slit and lapping him up. The sight of his beautiful wife before him, that luscious pink mouth on his cock, was so erotic, he almost came then. But he inhaled slowly, forcing himself to hold off the inevitable release, wanting to savor every moment. His hand cupped her head, fingers sliding through the luxurious silk of her chestnut hair.

She sucked him deep again, working him with her hand and her clever mouth. And when she withdrew to run her tongue along the bottom length while pumping him with the steady, smooth motions she knew he could not resist, he gave himself over to her completely.

No more protest.

"I surrender," he managed. "I am yours, Countess. Completely and utterly yours."

"Then come for me," she whispered, and took him down her throat again, so deep that when she swallowed, he could no longer withstand the furious need to spend.

With a surge and a cry, he filled her mouth with his release.

In the aftermath, she tucked him gently back into his trousers and rose elegantly to her feet.

"I shall see you at home, husband," she said cheerfully, as if she had not just shaken his world and it was every day that she surprised her husband with a visit and an orgasm that was still reverberating through him even now.

He rose from the chair with a growl. "To the devil with these ledgers. I'll have one of my men tend to the floor. I'm going home with you to finish what you've begun."

"Truly," she began, "there is no need…"

"There is every need," he corrected her. "If you recall from the first visit you paid this office, I am a man of action when presented with a challenge."

"If you insist," she said, grinning.

"I do." Bending, he scooped up his wife.

She laughed as her arms flew around his neck. He loved that sound. And he loved *her*.

Wolf Sutton was a damned lucky cove.

~

Dear reader,

Thank you for reading Wolf and Portia's love story! I hope you loved them every bit as much as I loved writing their happily ever after! Please read on for an excerpt from Lily's story, *Sutton's Scandal*! If you're wondering about Portia's friend Hattie, the Duchess of Montrose, you can find her story in *Duke of Debauchery*.

*Sutton's Scandal*
*The Sinful Suttons*
*Book Six*

Lily Sutton has been running wild for years beneath her siblings' noses. Born and raised in the rookeries, she is not afraid of anything or anyone. And she is most certainly not cowed by arrogant, heartless scoundrels like the owner of London's most prestigious shop, Bellingham and Co. She is determined to right the wrongs of her world, even if it means resorting to devious methods, such as absconding with some overpriced fripperies and baubles.

The illegitimate son of a duke, Tarquin Bellingham is intent upon earning his rightful place in society. His thriving shop and amassed wealth have at last afforded him the opportunity to marry a lady of good breeding. His sole irritation is the daring thief who continues to make a mockery of him. When he catches the tempting East End lady responsible, however, no one is more shocked by his reaction than Tarquin.

One mistake, and Lily finds herself at the mercy of a man who is as handsome as he is forbidding. His demand for repayment is outrageous. And absurdly enticing. Tarquin knows he should stay far away from a devious minx like Lily Sutton, but he can't seem to resist the lovely spitfire who has enchanted him against his will. But he doesn't dare risk the life he has struggled to build for a lady he can never trust, and Lily isn't about to surrender her freedom for a cold-hearted businessman...

### Chapter One

TARQUIN BELLINGHAM WAS AN IRRITATINGLY comely man.

'Twas a deuced pity he was also an insufferable arsehole.

It was the latter, rather than the former, which made stealing from him that much more satisfying, Lily Sutton thought to herself as she carefully slid a handsome fan down her bodice. The ivory handle glided smoothly beneath her chemise, resting cool and forbidden between her breasts. Yet another secret to add to the ever-mounting pile.

One day, she would repent her sins.

But first, there was that damned enticing pair of gloves dangling fortuitously near her left hand from its place upon the shelf...

"Miss Sutton?"

Lily started at the unexpected voice at her back and spun

about to find Mr. Smythe hovering in surprising proximity. The shop attendant was an obsequious cove if she'd ever met one. Always eager to please the patrons of the grand establishment that was Bellingham and Co. Easy to fool, just the way she preferred. But unless she was mistaken, there was a new hardness to his eyes and jaw this afternoon.

To his voice, as well.

She bestowed her best smile upon him. "Good afternoon, Mr. Smythe."

"Good afternoon, miss," he returned, looking distinctly uncomfortable. He shifted weight from one foot to the other, and then cleared his throat.

For the past several weeks, Lily had been making a regular jaunt to London's most prestigious shop. Bellingham and Co. boasted four different departments. Lily's favorite was furs and fans, because stuffing the costly goods to be had within its partitions was far easier than attempting certain others. Clocks, for instance. Bonnets, for another.

It was because of her frequent journeys from her family's gaming hell to Pall Mall that Lily had become quite familiar with Mr. Smythe by now. Their paths had crossed on numerous occasions. His demeanor on past excursions, however, had never seemed ominous as it did on this particular afternoon.

Something was amiss.

"What is troubling you, Mr. Smythe?" she asked kindly, keenly aware of the presence of her secreted fan. "Is it the weather? Dreadfully cold, with the portent of rain. Terribly grim, is it not?"

Lily was skilled at distraction. And deception, when the situation merited it.

Robbing Tarquin Bellingham's store of its trifles was one of those situations.

"I have been asked to bring you with me, Miss Sutton,"

Mr. Smythe said, his countenance forbidding as ever. Nary a hint of a welcoming smile as he extended his arm, as if to offer her escort.

Lily stared at Mr. Smythe's brown, woolen sleeve, the elbow crooked, and felt her guts twist and tighten into a knot. "And where do you intend to take me, sir?"

"I am to take you to Mr. Bellingham himself, miss." Mr. Smythe swallowed, the action making his Adam's apple bob above his simply tied neck cloth.

*Mr. Bellingham himself.*

Well, how do you do? The lofty Mr. Tarquin Bellingham, the owner of Bellingham and Co., the merciless scoundrel, wished an audience with Lily Sutton.

Without thought, her fingers lightly traced over her bodice above the fan she had so recently placed there, beneath the safe haven of her stays.

"Unfortunately, I don't wish to see Mr. Bellingham," she told Mr. Smythe, blunting the sting of her denial with a smile as she skirted around him to continue on her shopping excursion.

But Mr. Smythe was quicker-footed than he looked, moving to impede her further movement. "I am afraid the meeting is compulsory, Miss Sutton."

Her heart, which had slowed its pace as her initial surprise at Mr. Smythe's appearance, resumed a frantic pace once more.

"Compulsory," she repeated slowly, turning the word over on her tongue.

A large word for a man who believed himself far more important than all London. Of course he would issue such a decree. And as if she were Mr. Bellingham's grateful vassal, she was expected to follow Mr. Smythe to a place of his choosing.

"Yes, Miss Sutton," Mr. Smythe said, shifting again from

foot to foot as a dull, red flush stole over his cheekbones. "That was Mr. Bellingham's word."

She took pity on the poor cove, but not so much that she was going to leap into the air when Tarquin Bellingham told her to jump. "If you please, Mr. Smythe, inform Mr. Bellingham that I ain't his to order about. If you'll excuse me, I've a carriage awaiting me."

*And a stolen fan tickling my rib cage. I really must go before it unintentionally falls to the floor.*

Lily wisely kept that last to herself.

"But Miss Sutton..."

"That will be all, Mr. Smythe," said a cold, smooth-as-butter masculine voice.

And Mr. Smythe promptly scuttled away for the devil himself had arrived.

Lily felt his stare on her back before she turned to face him slowly, gracefully.

Elegantly.

Secretly praying the fan would not slide free and land at her feet.

And he was every bit as handsome as she recalled. Tall and imposing, with thick, dark hair and eyes that were more gray than blue. With a strong blade of a jaw and a proud chin. And a mouth that looked as if it had been sculpted by God for the sheer purpose of temptation. What a dreadful shame those lips were always held in such a tight, rigid line of disapproval. And what a waste for the rest of him to be every bit as bang up to the mark as his voice promised.

Because what was on the inside was rotten.

"Come with me, if you please, madam," Mr. Bellingham said curtly.

Lily held his stare, allowing all the defiant fire burning within to show. "No."

He raised a brow, his expression incredulous for a

moment so brief Lily thought she may have imagined it. "No?"

Perhaps it was a word—a concept, even—with which he was unfamiliar. Refusal. Denial. Being told no.

*Too bloody bad, Bellingham.*

"You heard me," she said agreeably. "No."

And with that calm pronouncement, Lily sidestepped Mr. Bellingham.

"Perhaps I ought to have been clearer." His hand shot out, staying her. "I was not asking, Miss Sutton. I was demanding."

Want more? Get *Sutton's Scandal*!

# AUTHOR'S NOTE

The cant speech used by the Suttons has been sourced mostly from *The Memoirs of James Hardy Vaux* (1819) and Grose's *Dictionary of the Vulgar Tongue* (1811).

# DON'T MISS SCARLETT'S OTHER ROMANCES!

Complete Book List
**HISTORICAL ROMANCE**

Heart's Temptation
A Mad Passion (Book One)
Rebel Love (Book Two)
Reckless Need (Book Three)
Sweet Scandal (Book Four)
Restless Rake (Book Five)
Darling Duke (Book Six)
The Night Before Scandal (Book Seven)

Wicked Husbands
Her Errant Earl (Book One)
Her Lovestruck Lord (Book Two)
Her Reformed Rake (Book Three)
Her Deceptive Duke (Book Four)
Her Missing Marquess (Book Five)
Her Virtuous Viscount (Book Six)

DON'T MISS SCARLETT'S OTHER ROMANCES!

League of Dukes
Nobody's Duke (Book One)
Heartless Duke (Book Two)
Dangerous Duke (Book Three)
Shameless Duke (Book Four)
Scandalous Duke (Book Five)
Fearless Duke (Book Six)

Notorious Ladies of London
Lady Ruthless (Book One)
Lady Wallflower (Book Two)
Lady Reckless (Book Three)
Lady Wicked (Book Four)
Lady Lawless (Book Five)
Lady Brazen (Book 6)

Unexpected Lords
The Detective Duke (Book One)
The Playboy Peer (Book Two)
The Millionaire Marquess (Book Three)

The Wicked Winters
Wicked in Winter (Book One)
Wedded in Winter (Book Two)
Wanton in Winter (Book Three)
Wishes in Winter (Book 3.5)
Willful in Winter (Book Four)
Wagered in Winter (Book Five)
Wild in Winter (Book Six)
Wooed in Winter (Book Seven)
Winter's Wallflower (Book Eight)
Winter's Woman (Book Nine)
Winter's Whispers (Book Ten)

DON'T MISS SCARLETT'S OTHER ROMANCES!

Winter's Waltz (Book Eleven)
Winter's Widow (Book Twelve)
Winter's Warrior (Book Thirteen)

The Sinful Suttons
Sutton's Spinster (Book One)
Sutton's Sins (Book Two)
Sutton's Surrender (Book Three)
Sutton's Seduction (Book Four)
Sutton's Scoundrel (Book Five)
Sutton's Scandal (Book Six)
Sutton's Secrets (Book Seven)

Sins and Scoundrels
Duke of Depravity
Prince of Persuasion
Marquess of Mayhem
Sarah
Earl of Every Sin
Duke of Debauchery

Second Chance Manor
The Matchmaker and the Marquess by Scarlett Scott
The Angel and the Aristocrat *by Merry Farmer*
The Scholar and the Scot *by Caroline Lee*
The Venus and the Viscount by Scarlett Scott
The Buccaneer and the Bastard *by Merry Farmer*
The Doxy and the Duke *by Caroline Lee*

Stand-alone Novella
Lord of Pirates

**CONTEMPORARY ROMANCE**

DON'T MISS SCARLETT'S OTHER ROMANCES!

Love's Second Chance
Reprieve (Book One)
Perfect Persuasion (Book Two)
Win My Love (Book Three)

Coastal Heat
Loved Up (Book One)

## ABOUT THE AUTHOR

*USA Today* and Amazon bestselling author Scarlett Scott writes steamy Victorian and Regency romance with strong, intelligent heroines and sexy alpha heroes. She lives in Pennsylvania and Maryland with her Canadian husband, adorable identical twins, and two dogs.

A self-professed literary junkie and nerd, she loves reading anything, but especially romance novels, poetry, and Middle English verse. Catch up with her on her website https://scarlettscottauthor.com. Hearing from readers never fails to make her day.

Scarlett's complete book list and information about upcoming releases can be found at https://scarlettscottauthor.com.

Connect with Scarlett! You can find her here:
  Join Scarlett Scott's reader group on Facebook for early excerpts, giveaways, and a whole lot of fun!
  Sign up for her newsletter here
  https://www.tiktok.com/@authorscarlettscott

- facebook.com/AuthorScarlettScott
- twitter.com/scarscoromance
- instagram.com/scarlettscottauthor
- bookbub.com/authors/scarlett-scott
- amazon.com/Scarlett-Scott/e/B004NW8N2I
- pinterest.com/scarlettscott

Printed in Dunstable, United Kingdom